DARK CURSE

Guardians of the Fae Realms: Book 6
JL Madore

Dark Curse: Guardians of the Fae Realms

JL Madore -- 1st ed.

ISBN: 978-1-998372-63-8

BEFORE YOU START!

Dark Curse is book one in Nakeyla Northwood's harem and book 6 in the universe of The Guardians of the Fae Realms. If you missed the first harem and the intro to how we got here, start at book 1 of the entire series as this story is a continuation of plot and cast of character from the first group of lovers.

Guardians of the Phoenix.

If you don't want to, that's fine too, I've given a recap in the first pages so you get the gist of what you missed.

Enjoy,

JL

CHAPTER ONE

Keyla

*T*here's something carnal about a man working in the outdoors, shirt off, muscled body glistening in the sunlight of an autumn morning. Any hot-blooded female would stop to admire a well-built male but when that male is yours—well, almost yours—it's even better. As a fae wildling, my blood runs hotter than most.

The raw power of Doc's abs and pecs tensing and releasing as he pushes a saw through boards or drives nails into wood with his hammer is beyond titillating.

He knows how to use a hammer.

My heart stumbles behind my ribs as the heat of my gaze triggers his bear's instincts and he turns so our gazes lock.

My wolf stirs.

My body warms.

My determination grows.

The heat in those dark hazel eyes is a tangible caress—a promise for later when we're alone. Dark and intimate is our specialty. I've come to count on our stolen moments.

I want him—all of him.

We haven't had sex or mated yet because life has been hectic with Kotah and his mates fulfilling their quest to open the Portal Gate—but soon.

He loves me and I love him.

"Nakeyla Northwood, eyes front." I jump at the cold snap of my mother's censure and straighten to face her in our fireside circle. "The pedestrian behavior of your brother and his commoner mates will *not* rub off on you. You are the Prime Princess for goddess sake. Act like it."

I fix my gaze across the forest clearing and try not to think about the male at work behind me.

"I was admiring the progress of the construction, Mother. Hawk's team has worked feverishly since Calli opened the Portal Gate. In a mere twenty-four hours, they've built the infrastructure of a permanent gate site, not to mention basic cabins for temporary lodgings. I, for one, am pleased Calli doesn't have to sleep in a tent again tonight. Especially now that she's pregnant."

Mother frowns. "Wooden boxes with no furnishings are not accommodations befitting the royal family. Your brother doesn't understand a thing about his station. Your father would have never allowed us to be forced to sleep in a forest."

I fight not to laugh. "We are *wolf* wildlings. A forest is where our animal sides belong."

"You forget your place, Nakeyla."

No. I don't. It's she who has forgotten. Too much time spent in a palace has consumed the joy of wind blowing through her fur as her claws dig into the pithy ground. I gaze at the vibrant golds and oranges and reds of the turning leaves and wonder how she can be here and not celebrate the stunning perfection of nature.

But she doesn't. All she wants is to return to the splendor of the Prime Palace and stride up the halls so people can bow and move out of her way.

"How long do you think it will be before the gate is functional and we can make contact with the fae on the other side?" I ask.

She runs a hand over the silk of her tattered and sullied coronation gown and arches a manicured brow. "From what Nakotah said, it depends on the people of StoneHaven. Once they complete the preparations in the other realm, a bridge between the two civilizations will be established."

"It's an exciting time."

"A dangerous time, you mean. After centuries of being cut off from our fae counterparts, we have no idea what might come through that portal. Caution should have been the priority, not haste."

The disapproval in her tone is heavy-handed. She didn't support the quest to open the rift to the Fae Realm. In fact, there is evidence to suggest she might've even acted against Kotah and his mates on their quest.

I refuse to get caught up in politics or her negativity.

After months of worrying about Kotah, Calli, Jaxx, Hawk, and Brant, they finally pieced together their destiny and opened the portal to the other fae realm.

A lot of people doubted they could do it.

Honestly, there were times I worried they might not be able do it. It was a struggle from the start. Calli was an unskilled human, with no particular talents other than surviving a difficult life, and no knowledge of our world.

Then she was killed in a car chase, resurrected as the Fae Phoenix, and then guys bonded as her Guardians.

Despite the views of skeptics and nay-sayers, they battled the opposing forces, cut through the political bullcrap of the Fae Council, my parents, and Hawk's father, and united the two realms.

I don't suppose all those battles are over.

Hawk's half-brother, Hunter, hasn't been caught and there are still so many questions about what he and Sebastian White-house Senior were trying to accomplish.

"Like it or not, the Portal Gate will soon be a functioning part of Kotah's legacy to the realm. I, for one, think it's wonder-ful. I'm very proud of him."

"Yes, well, you are young and know no better."

"I'll be twenty in a matter of weeks. In civilizations past, I would already be married with several litters of pups by now."

If it weren't so pedestrian, my mother would be rolling her eyes at me.

The throaty *chuff, chuff, chuff* of helicopter rotors draws my gaze to the sky. "How many more trips do you think Hawk's people will make to finish construction?"

"I'm sure I don't know. Let us hope the bag I requested from the palace is among the contents so I can get out of this dress."

"You look resplendent as always, Mother. And if your things didn't make it to join the shipment, Calli offered you a change of clothes. The guys always pack her a few extra slip dresses for after she flames out."

The tsking hiss that escapes my mother's lips is pure horror. "A slip dress? What am I, a streetwalker?"

How we got from slip dress to prostitution, I'll never know and I don't want to. I follow the flight of the helicopter over the clearing toward where it will land on the other side of the river.

Oh, lovely. My line of sight has now brought me back to Doc, glistening with hard work.

I honestly could watch him all day.

"Speaking of streetwalkers. Your hormones betray you, daughter. While forced to live like common folk, you've forgotten your station and breeding. How do you think it makes me look when people see you salivating over a half-naked male."

I draw a deep breath and try to find my inner Zen. "There's

no need to work yourself up, Mother. I haven't forgotten how to behave. How could I? You remind me with such regularity."

Mother pins me with one of her notoriously piercing glares. "And yet you continue to admire the physique of that bear. It will stop, child. And it will stop now."

"I'm sure I don't know what you're talking about, and if I did, I would remind you his name is Doc, not 'that bear'."

"*Doc* is a layman commentary on the male's hobby, not his name."

"Fine, his name is Doctor Dillan Baskins, and being a doctor isn't his hobby, Mother. He was an emergency medic in the military and when he returned to civilian life, he earned his doctorate to practice medicine."

"Being a small-town physician hardly qualifies him to court the sister of the Fae Prime. He's a beta for goddess sake."

I sigh, unsure how much more family time I'm going to be able to withstand. Kotah is chatting with Jaxx by the trees. After a few seconds of focusing my gaze on him, he turns and I send a plea for rescue.

Sitting straight on the wooden bench set by the fire, it's hard to feel like a royal. I rather enjoy the informality. It's got Mother all twisted up in pomp and pretense.

"A compromise then," I say, offering her a smile. "I will endeavor to be more discreet with my admirations in public if you endeavor to be civil to the common folk. I am a grown woman and enjoy spending time with Dillan. He is a strong and honorable male and I would very much like for you to get to know him."

Mother lets off a feminine note of derision and holds her hand out to study her polished nails. "You are a far cry from grown, child. You are a teenager swept away by a low-class rake who doesn't know the first thing about what it means to be royal."

Oh, my birthday can't come soon enough. To be rid of her

'teenager' insult will be my only birthday wish. "Well, Kotah likes him. Don't you, brother?" I extend my hand and Kotah helps me up. "And since *he* is the highest-ranking royal, I suppose that should settle it."

My brother releases my hand when I'm on my feet and reaches across my back to squeeze my shoulder. "Who do I like, little sister?"

"Doc." I frown and turn to our mother. "Apologies... I mean, Dillan. Mother doesn't think a military warrior turned doctor is a suitable courtier for me."

"His father was a blacksmith." Mother whispers the words as if the occupation is a shameful sin.

Kotah offers her a patient gaze. "Our community is strengthened by the diversity of its members, Mother. Without tradesmen, the realm would cease to function. A blacksmith is as important as a member of the palace staff or an executive of the Fae Concealment Office or a member of the royal family. We all play our part."

Mother's face is as cold and blank as always. "The fact you think so, child, is either due to you being coronated the Fae Prime days ago or fundamental flaws in your teaching."

Kotah's smile tightens, but he stands tall beneath the weight of judgment. He raises his hand and gestures for Raven to come forward.

Mother's personal assistant is never far, always waiting in the wings in case she's called upon.

"Thank you for your concern, Mother," he says, offering Raven a kind smile. "If you'll excuse us, I must speak with Keyla about another matter. Raven, would you mind keeping the Past Prima company?"

"Of course, Highness."

Tightening his grip on my shoulder, Kotah turns us toward the clearing, and we make our escape.

"My hero." I tilt my head to the side and rest it on Kotah's shoulder. With less than a year between us and parents more interested in realm politics than their children, he and I have depended on one another to navigate royal life.

"I shall always be your rescue."

The two of us stroll to the edge of the forest and he tilts his head toward the shade of the trees. "Do you fancy getting your claws dirty?"

"Do you have time? Aren't you in talks with the Pixie Queen?"

"Hawk excused me for a moment. We're playing good wolf/bad hawk and he asked me to step away for fifteen minutes."

"Well, that's the best offer I've had all morning." I consider the timeframe and gauge how far we can go. "Alright, I'll race you to the large boulder we found yesterday at the bend in the river. Do you remember?"

He grins and bends, ready to launch. "Let the race begin, little sister."

My claws tear into the stiff soil of the Pennsylvanian forest as Kotah and I dodge the rough-barked trees and pitted ground littered with a layered mosaic of fallen leaves. In our haste to reach the bend in the river, we scare up a rabbit, two grouse, and a bunch of chipmunks.

On another day, we might chase them down and hunt. Not today. This run is about abandoning the world and letting our wolves ascend.

The pithy ground of summer is tightening with the onset of frosty mornings but it still offers great traction. I propel myself forward on a high that I only get when in my wolf form.

This is me, world. Take it or leave it.

In a life where who I was born determines who I am as a

female, in my wolf form, only one truth exists—I am a wildling. I am wolf.

To have Kotah with me makes it even better.

He's the only one who truly understands. He is my strength and my home. For however long I can be a fundamental part of his life, I will relish it.

He's mated now... and expecting a pup.

My footing falters and I have to catch myself in a lunge to regain my pace. His new life is upon him. As much as it hurts to be left behind, things must change.

He has a new family now.

The acrid scent of heartache fills my heightened senses and I cut off my self-indulgence before Kotah smells it. Luckily, he's ahead of me and upwind.

I can't help feeling territorial.

Before Kotah's mating, I was his only love and the only one who loved him back for who he is. Now he has four mates who will die for him and who he loves beyond measure.

And I'm happy for him.

Truly.

Still. Where does that leave me?

I agreed to be his right hand running the realm largely for that reason. It is a place in his life where I can contribute to a level that keeps me relevant.

I shake my muzzle and try to clear my head.

I'm in wolf form and, for this moment, Kotah is mine. We're bolting through the trees, air rushing past us, ruffling our thick coats. Live in the moment, Keyla.

This is a very exciting time and there's no telling what destiny has in store for us all.

~

Creed

Sleep is so fucking evasive some nights. Lying naked in the bed I've had since I was old enough to be out of a crib, I stare up at the gold gilded ceiling. I should feel at home. This is *my* home. And yet some bitch hijacked it and is holding us all for ransom. I've tried to escape. I've tried to attack. I've tried to undermine her with the members of the royal staff who defected.

Maybe they think there's no going back. That the usurper Queen Laryssa will slaughter them all before she lets the crown be stripped from her head.

That's true. She would.

I could shut her down if I had my powers. If her torture ended, I could call the protectorate of the royal house and things would be different.

Assuming any of them still live.

But I can't call them to arms. I don't have my powers and I don't know where Laryssa has my sister and my mother held prisoner.

If I step out of line, they pay.

I close my eyes against the darkness and remind myself about what happened the last time I tried to escape. I made it out of the castle and into the labyrinth that lines three of the four sides of the castle.

While no one could track me through the warren of twists and turns that once stood as my childhood playground, the dragons flew over, sniffed me out, and dragged me back.

I expected a beating or her calling the beast she cursed me with to perform some horrific act. If only that were the case. My punishment was more soul-shattering than I could've imagined.

Instead of a brutal flogging, Laryssa ordered me to be chained to the wall of the dining hall to watch as her guards dragged my sister in kicking and screaming, and raped her.

That black-hearted menace to my quadrant forced me to watch as three men hurt and defiled her.

Laryssa reminds me often enough that it was *my* doing. She says if I simply comply with her wishes nothing like that needs to happen again.

And so I stopped trying to escape.

I stopped fighting the effects of the witch's curse.

I stopped trying to take back what is rightfully and legally mine.

But I'll never stop imagining the ways I will kill her.

If the Fates give me the opportunity, Laryssa is as good as dead—brutally, mercilessly, extinguished from this world.

A sliver of golden light slices the darkness on the far side of the suite as my dragon guard makes a surprise bed inspection. Vikarus and Rhylan Silverwing—the only two people allowed to interact with me within this private wing of the castle.

To the outside world, I became a recluse after my throne was taken and the two of them are my trusted bodyguards. In truth, they are my jailors.

"Not sleeping?" Rhy asks, stepping inside the door.

"No."

"It's late."

"I'm aware."

"Your back aching again?"

"No."

"You know I can smell the lie, right?"

Stupid wildling sense of smell. "You know I hate you, right?"

"You are in a mood." He closes the door, locking us in together. "You know I'm—"

"Save it. I don't have the patience tonight." The beast I've been cursed with is restless tonight. It claws at me, fighting to shift and take control. I refuse to give in.

Each time I give in, I lose a bit more of my soul.

If I don't hold the creature back, it will consume me. Some nights I worry if I fall asleep I'll never wake up.

With the door shut tight, I lose track of Rhy in the darkness.

I don't have night vision like wildlings do. I have the bastardized vision of the beast but I don't activate that. That gives the thing power.

I worry it might also allow the queen and the blood witch who cursed me the ability to see what I see. I don't know for sure, but I wouldn't put it past them.

"The curse bothering you tonight?"

"It's a curse. When doesn't it bother me?"

Over the past two years, I learned without fail that Vik is a dick and Rhy will lie.

Maybe it's childish to think of them that way, but it helps me remember they aren't my friends. We might go along with the act when I'm being dragged out to perform in public, but it's just that—an act.

I'm their prisoner—the queen's trophy.

Sometimes I think there's more to Rhylan. When held up in comparison with his twin, Rhy is the more pleasant male. But more pleasant only goes so far when the baseline starts with a miserable, arrogant prick.

I track the sound of his movement through my suite and when the light goes on in my ensuite washroom, I roll my eyes. We've danced this dance more than once. "I'm not in the mood for this tonight, Dragon."

"Uh-huh." The sound of him taking a piss cuts off before the water runs and he opens the cabinet over my hand basin. When he returns, he leaves on the washroom light but closes the door all but a few inches. "Roll over."

"Seriously not in the mood."

"Then get in the mood because we're headed out in a few hours and you need to get some rest."

I growl and glare. "Headed out where?"

He stops at the side of my bed and swirls his finger in the universal signal for me to roll over. He's not going to tell me anything if I don't comply, so I give in.

"You're an asshole."

"Without a doubt." He runs his fingers across my shoulder blades and plows my hair to the side. I'll never admit it, but the man's got great hands. When my phantom wings hurt this bad, only Rhy can make it stop.

The medicated massage oil is cool on my heated back and I tense as he starts to rub it in.

Yet another reason to kill the Bitch Queen Laryssa. She had one of her men butcher my wings off so I couldn't fly away. I'm a faery with no fucking wings.

How messed up is that?

After a few moments, the numbing agent in the oil takes hold and the throbbing ache begins to dissipate. I can breathe again.

Despite me hating everything about this situation, I can't help but moan and sink deeper into my mattress. Sometimes you don't realize how much pain you're in until it lessens.

"Better?" Rhy asks, spreading more on and really working it in under my shoulder blades where the cartilage was shorn.

As arrogant as it sounds, I used to enjoy my body and dazzling the ladies when naked. No longer. What kind of faery prince has no wings?

The citizens don't realize it yet, because our wings aren't out until we extend them for flight or battle, but one day someone will figure it out and I'll be ousted as a laughingstock.

Rhy is the only person who's seen the damage. Not because I invited him to—no—the dragon is as stubborn as he is misguided.

"Shit, you really are worked up tonight. Your muscles are solid rock."

"You can leave at any time."

"Not until I'm sure you'll get a few hours' sleep."

"I'm a puppet. I can perform on no sleep."

"Not gonna happen. You've still got time to rest."

The tone in his voice is verging on sounding like he cares, and I can't take it. I roll out from under his touch and get some distance. "You know where the door is."

"I do but I'm not leaving. I haven't gotten what I came for." Still sitting on the edge of my bed, he unclips the buckles on his boots and shucks off his pants. Next is his shirt and he's strolling toward me, his fists up. "You need to work off some of this fighting spirit, my prince."

"I'm not your prince, asshole."

"Then come prove me wrong."

Such an asshole.

He grabs the bottle of massage oil off the bedstand and squeezes some into his cupped hand. Reaching behind his back, he widens his stance and makes a show of rubbing it against his ass. "Come and get it. If you're man enough. Fuck the man who fucks you over. Fair's fair, right?"

"Not interested."

His mouth curves in a cocky grin. "Your cock says different."

I glance down at the traitorous organ and grunt. I'm hard and standing firmly in anticipation, my cock pointing straight at what it's throbbing for. "Doesn't mean I have to do anything about it."

Rhy dips his chin and gives me a half-hooded gaze. "Enemies with benefits. Isn't that what you call us?"

There's no us. He's just my enemy. I know that.

His slow stalk toward me brings out all my defensive anxiety. "I hate you and everything you stand for."

"So you've said. I am clear where you stand."

When he gets close, I use both hands to shove him back. He recovers quickly and comes at me again. "One of these days, I'll tell your twin the kind of depraved fuckery we get up to. That duty-bound ass-kisser will lose his shit, you know he will."

"You're not telling anyone. If you did, you'd have to explain how it all started."

My right cross flies between us, but the bastard expects it. He ducks and chuckles. "That's right. Come and get me. Your cock gets so brutally hard when your blood is pumping."

I spin, lifting my heel to catch his side and he grabs my leg. Fighting your sparring partner makes fighting less effective. The two of us let loose, me throwing punches and coming at him hard and him blocking and rendering my assaults useless.

Story of my fucking life.

On a spin, I grab his wrist and swing around to elbow him in the face. The crunch of cartilage is so fucking satisfying my cock weeps.

Rhy steps back, resets his nose, and grins. The stupid fucker has wildling healing. It's already knitting back together as the blood's still warm on his lips.

"Nice one," he says, pointing down at my cock. "Want me to help with that? You've sprung a leak."

I launch forward, my fist whistling past his ear as he ducks. It's a wonder he can see me coming with his mop of golden hair in front of his eyes.

Punch after punch, he diverts my power, grinning, the piercing in his cock catching the light now and then and drawing my attention. Fuck me, I love the feel of that steel ball.

Cum is tingling deep in my balls and the pressure behind it is building. It's the most messed up foreplay ever and I'm ashamed it gets me off.

But it does.

Fuck yeah, it does.

My breath is coming hard and fast when I give up on the assault and grip my cock, tugging to prime it good and hard. "Same rules."

"Same rules. Punish me as long and as rough as you need and when you're done, I walk out that door and it never happened."

"Grip the footboard."

He surrenders without hesitation. Facing the solid slab of

carved walnut, he grips the bed frame and gives me a glorious view of his ass.

Damn him. He's right. I need this. I grip my shaft and sweep the engorged tip through the oil he set in place. With one hand on the bone of his hip, I thrust forward and breach the constriction.

Rhy tenses and lets off a hiss.

Yes, I could do the whole ease inside inch-by-inch thing and get some glide going before I penetrate him fully but why. This is punishment, after all.

"Brace yourself."

Doc

"You're going to kink your neck craning it around to check out the forest every five minutes. Have a little dignity man. She'll be back when she's back."

I meet Lukas's amused gaze and hold the circular saw in my hand blade up and pointed at him. "Never diss the man with the steel teeth."

To emphasize my point, I pull the trigger and the whine of the motor lets off a screeching squeal.

Lukas chuckles, holding up his palms. "Don't let me disturb you, Bear. I came over to let you know the next delivery of supplies landed. We've got men unpacking the crates now."

I set the saw down and jump off the platform of the cabin we're working on. We've got four almost boxed up and this would be the fifth. They're nothing fancy yet but it's a roof and four walls.

"Did we get the plywood and planks I asked for?"

"They're listed on the manifest, but we won't know for sure until they get things opened and inventoried. With Jayne on the other end, though, I'd be surprised if things aren't accurate."

Good. That's good.

The two of us tromp the short distance to where Hawk's men are dropping the wooden crates at the edge of the trees. I grab a pry bar and start removing the lids of a couple of shipping crates. Peering in, I start to mentally inventory what we've got to work with.

Despite being a stubborn, billionaire dick at times, Hawk gets things done. The man is on top of the totem pole for a reason.

"Calli, one sec." Lukas calls over Calli and Jaxx as the lovely couple stroll through the clearing. The two of them make a beautiful blonde Barbie and Ken image. That is if Barbie could burst into a fiery phoenix and Ken was a cowboy who morphed into a spank, vicious jaguar.

Lukas pulls a box out of the crate he's going through and points at the picture on the front of the packaging. "I believe this was purchased with you in mind."

Calli grins from ear to ear and holds it up for Jaxx to see. "A memory foam mattress. Just what I wanted."

Jaxx chuckles. "That's our avian. Always anticipating our needs. Come on, let's take it to the tent and get it set up."

"Forget the tent." I point back the way they came toward the construction area. "It's not much, but we have the first two tiny houses framed and sided. You're welcome to claim one and get off the forest floor."

Brant comes loping out of the trees, his brown curls swaying against his broad shoulders. My bear brother has his hands cupped and overflowing with berries. "Did I hear you say we have walls and a door?"

"And a comfy foam topper," Calli adds, showing him her box while waggling her hips.

"Booyah! Lead the way, my brother. Let's check out the new digs."

Jaxx chuckles. "And when you say check out…"

My eyes roll as I turn to lead the way. "We all know what he means. Just keep in mind that we've got workers busily building temporary lodgings right next door. We don't want to hear your throaty throes of orgasm."

Brant snorts. "Then hammer and saw as loud as you can and you won't hear us. Otherwise… orgasms baby."

I shake my head. The guy will never change. "Keyla and I thought Calli might want to rest. You know… because she was so tired yesterday and that was before the day went to shit."

Calli's cheeks pink up. "And before you all found out I'm preggers."

I shrug. "I wasn't sure if you knew yet. Keyla smelled it in your scent yesterday, but she said it's very faint. I can't smell it at all."

Brant grins and holds his cupped hands up for Calli to select a few berries. "The wolves for the olfactory win. Kotah smelled it too."

I pat Brant's shoulder and point to the framed box on the edge of the treeline. "Then let me congratulate you all on your cub. It's amazing news. This is you. Enjoy. And I promise we'll hammer loudly."

Calli looks at Brant and her cheeks flush hot pink. "So much for taking a nap. Now they're going to intentionally make noise."

Jaxx laughs as the three of them duck inside.

Good for them. I've never seen Brant so happy and it looks good on him. He's come a long way from the orphaned bear I fostered with back on the ranch.

I leave the three of them to have their fun and head back to the tiny house I was working on before. Hawk's men have started stacking lumber close by, so we're in good shape for a long afternoon of manual labor.

I'm about to reclaim my hammer and make some noise when I feel the heat of a gaze on me and turn.

Oh, fuck.

It's the Fae Prima—well, the former Fae Prima—Keyla's mom. When she gives me the royal come hither finger curl, my bowels pretty much liquefy.

Straightening, I grab a rag off the platform and wipe my hands. Why does the former Queen of the Realm want to speak to me? There is literally only one reason and I already know it won't be good.

Cue the 'you aren't good enough for my daughter' speech. Shit. I knew it would come. Things were going too well between Keyla and me for it not to.

"Prima," I drop my gaze and offer her the respect a woman in her position deserves. "Good afternoon, Majesty. You want to speak to me?"

The similarities between the Fae Prima and her children are unmistakable. Both Kotah and Keyla have the same long, chestnut hair, warm, coppery skin, and rich brown eyes as their mother and their native heritage.

But the differences between them are equally unmistakable. Kotah and Keyla have a warm smile, an open heart, and respect for others their mother doesn't.

"In truth, Mr. Baskins, I don't want to speak with you at all. Yet here we are."

Okaaay, awesome start.

I've learned from watching Keyla and her brother when speaking to their mother it's best to say nothing until you're drawn into the convo with a question.

I fold my hands at my back and assume the position.

I'm not an overly tall male when compared to Brant, Hawk,

or even Lukas, but I'm built like the soldier I have always been and carry the bulk and strength of my bear over a large frame.

I'm not a pushover by any means.

Malayna Northwood stands a foot shorter than me, almost a hundred pounds lighter and, for reals, she intimidates the piss out of me.

"You have work to do, Mr. Baskins, so let me be frank and not waste our time. You are in no way a suitable match for my daughter. You seem fairly intelligent, so I assume you already know that."

I blink. "Keyla is an extremely special lady—"

"—not a lady." She waggles her finger in the air between us. "Nakeyla is a nineteen-year-old child who has no experience with males and has lived a sheltered life. Her infatuation with you is understandable, you are an adequate-looking, strapping male, but as the adult in the mix, I expect you to realize she deserves better."

I force a smile and choose my words carefully. "I respect what you're saying, Prima, and yes, I considered our positions in life. The truth is, I'm a soldier who served with honor and then became a doctor. I live my life to a standard and hold myself to a code. When I spoke to your son about courting Keyla—"

"My son?" She dips her chin, and her lips tighten.

I realize giving Kotah consideration over her is a mistake a moment too late. Danger. Danger.

A glance toward the trees offers me no escape. Where is everyone when you need a rescue? There's no way out of this so I suck it up and try again.

"I hear what you're saying, Prima, and I respect your position and your concerns. Rest assured, I'll give it more thought and speak to your daughter about it."

She lifts her chin and there's no doubt that I have been dismissed.

Alrighty then. Good talk.

I bend at the waist as I retreat with my tail tucked between my legs and a demoralizing sense of what it feels like to be a neutered male.

CHAPTER TWO

Keyla

*T*he midday sun is almost directly overhead, casting off an unseasonable warmth for an autumn day. Eyes closed and face lifted to the sky, I'm sunning myself on a large rock like a lazy cat, daydreaming about my boyfriend and what he looks like with and without clothing.

Doc is gorgeous with tanned skin, vibrant hazel eyes, and midnight black hair that is as dark as his bear's lush coat. He has a thickly muscled body and wears jeans and tight t-shirts that hide nothing of his strength.

I hear him coming long before I would ever hear a wolf. Twigs snap under the thick tread of his boots and the rhythmic *thump, thump,* of the earth accepting his weight vibrates in gentle tremors beneath me.

Bears are a different breed than wolves—that's for certain—but even for a bear, Doc's footfalls are heavy.

I guess my time for outdoor indulgence is over.

Shifting to face the trees, it takes a moment for my eyes to adjust. I find Doc approaching in the shadows and try to gauge what happened since I saw him not two hours ago.

The moment he's close enough for me to read his expression I know I won't like what's coming. "What's wrong? Did something happen with Calli? Did you fight with Brant?"

He shakes his head and gestures for me to scoot over and give him room to join me on my rock. "Nothing like that. Everything's fine. I'm just bagged from two days of building. I'm giving myself a much-deserved break."

I don't doubt that's true, but I smell the lie even before it's out of his mouth. It hits me then. Of course, it's her. Her comments about me dating the son of a blacksmith still hang in the air and now he looks like someone kicked him in the crotch and his parts are all knotted up.

"Please tell me you aren't listening to anything my mother says."

The way he gathers my hand and sighs, I know I'm right and the poison is spreading.

I shift on the hard surface and face him.

"You can't possibly be listening to her objections. I warned you about what she's like. We've had endless conversations about how she twists people up to get what she wants. She's a professional manipulator."

He scrubs his hand over the dark scruff of his jaw and exhales. "I'm aware of what your mother wants and why. It doesn't mean we should ignore her worries."

"Yes, it does. Ignoring my mother's protestations is exactly what we should do."

"Keyla, listen to me—"

Shaking my head, I hold up a finger "No. You listen to me. She chose her mate for status and power. Theirs was an arrangement of two driven, like-minded people. They cared for each other and possibly that grew to love, but that's not what I want."

He squeezes my fingers and brings them to his mouth to kiss my knuckles. "How can you truly know what you want? You're young and have been sheltered in the palace with people treading lightly around you..."

As he regurgitates my mother's corruption, my mind fritzes. Young and naïve. Yes, there it is. I'm young and inexperienced so how could I possibly know my own body and mind.

My heart withers a little under the judgment.

I launch off the rock to stand my ground. My steps are quick and heavy as I pace toward a wide-trunked tree and then double back. "Don't act the part of her puppet. It's beneath you and frankly, I'm disappointed."

Anguish flares in his eyes. "I'm not. It wouldn't bother me if it wasn't true."

I cross my arms over my chest and ready for what's next. "If you're ending us, do it. I may be young, but I'm not a child. I'll take it on the chin and it'll be done."

He rushes forward and squeezes my elbows looking stricken. "End us? Fuck, no. I'm not ending us."

"Then what is this? One conversation alone with my mother and I don't know my own mind? Give me some credit. Do you truly think that little of me?"

His bear lets off a growl and he glares at the sunny sky. "I'm fucking this up."

"Agreed."

He meets my heated gaze and the agony in those eyes presses on my lungs. "I give you *all* the credit, Keyla. You're cultured and beautiful and educated and understand the politics and the importance of realm life enough to assist the leader of our world. You amaze me every fucking day."

"Yet I'm too immature to know my heart?"

He curses and closes his hands into fists. "I'm just worried about us mating before you know more. I'm eight years older, have traveled the world with the military, and have had more experiences than most."

"Sexually, you mean."

His face drops and the stench of guilt oozes off him. "You haven't had those opportunities. Maybe there's someone who is better for you and I'm selfish to want to claim you before you've had a chance to find him."

Unbelievable. "So, I should venture out into the world and sleep with men and test our love to see if what we have is real? Do you hear how stupid that sounds?"

"I'm not saying I want that. I *don't.*"

I stare at the river and try to recapture the peace I felt before he got here. No luck. "Do you think Brant gave Kotah this speech?"

"What? Why ask me that?"

"Because my brother and I are less than a year apart in age and you and Brant share much the same history. Do you think your bear brother accused my brother of being too naïve to know his heart? Do you think he put him off and rejected him in his bed for Kotah's own good? Or is it different because he's male?"

He scowls. "Don't do that. This is about you and me. Don't bring other people into the equation."

"Like you did when you asked Kotah if he would give us his blessing before you'd date me? Didn't *that* bring other people into the equation?"

He steps back and sighs. "Babe, I'm sorry. I apologized for that. I admit I don't know how to do this, and I've made some mistakes but give me a break. Dating you isn't easy."

That hurts. "You're saying *I'm* the problem?"

He kicks at the dirt and curses, the stress of this conversation visible in the rigidity of his broad shoulders. "Like it or not, you are Nakeyla-fucking-Northwood and you are the Prime

Princess. You're the realm's sweetheart. You're a beloved royal. That's a lot to live up to."

"Forget my status. I'm a girl who wants to be seen and heard and loved. Why is that difficult?"

"It's not. Loving you is as easy as breathing. And I *do* love you. You are my heart and my every waking thought and my bear feels the same way."

I groan. "Then why are we fighting?"

He draws a deep breath and exhales, forcing a smile. "I'm trying to do right by you. My bear and I want you forever and always. That's a lock. If it was only you and me in this world, I would've mated you months ago."

"You should have."

His expression eases a little as his forced smile becomes a relaxed smirk. "Our months together have been about Kotah and Brant and all their Guardian drama. I want our mating to be about us. No pending attacks. No Black Knight trying to take over the realm. No corporate corruption."

"And now that all that is over, instead of claiming me—as we both want—you think I should date other men? That's the opposite of what I want."

He sighs. "I only aired your options because I want to discuss things and make sure you're sure. I never want you to regret mating me."

I run my fingers through my hair and groan.

How can such a smart man be so stupid? Shaking my hands out at my side helps the tingling of my skin a bit but I still want to jump him and punch his sexy face.

Not very royal behavior, but my wolf's first instinct is to strike out when people hurt us. Instead of going with the impulse, I suppress my wolf and rein in control.

This entire conversation is, after all, about whether I'm adult enough to make good decisions.

I am.

I draw a deep breath and exhale. "Let me give you a tip you'd do well to commit to memory. Are you ready?"

He nods, looking somewhat terrified. "Uh-huh."

"Other people have decided my life for me since before I was born—parents, governesses, servants, tutors, council members, the list goes on. They deemed what I wore, how I should act, what I knew, where I lived, who was good enough to play with me. I hated it."

I grip his chin and hold his gaze locked with mine. "Don't think for me, Bear. Don't negate my voice. Trust me to know my mind. I'm not looking for an escort in life, or a guardian, or a protector. I want a partner. If you can't be that—"

"—I can," he snaps, his gaze darker than usual. "I *am* that person. Your mother got in my head and twisted me up because a part of me knows I'll never be good enough for you. I'm sorry."

I roll my eyes. "If your bar for greatness is the fact that I was born into a celebrity family—reevaluate it. I want to be measured based on my merit, not my DNA."

He opens his arms and I feel the pull of his bear's need to hold me. I need that too. I give in without protest and he wraps me within his strong embrace.

Pressing my face into the soft flesh of his neck, I soak in his warmth and breathe him in. Doc's scent calls to my wolf. It's musk and spruce with a hint of sunshine. It's a heady scent. "Please don't listen to my mother."

"Never again. I promise."

Good. That's good. With that settled I lean back and smile up at him. "Now, if you insist I'm better than you because I speak five languages and am in the top two percent of the population for IQ, that's a different story altogether."

He laughs. "Point made, babe. You being a princess is the

luck of sperm. You're too good for me for a slew of other reasons."

I lean forward and nip his bottom lip. "Crude, but accurate."

Doc

I lift Keyla off her feet, pulling her close to brush my lips against the silk of her cheek. She wraps her arms around my neck and her legs around my hips. She's tiny but mighty, my love—and that was our first real fight.

I exhale a heavy breath and try to ease my bear.

Keyla is ours. She chose us. We won't let her slip through our fingers. We're neither stupid enough nor altruistic enough to question our good fortune twice.

My bear growls his agreement and I claim her mouth in earnest. This is *not* a mistake. I will live and die holding myself to a standard she'll be proud of.

I sweep my tongue along the seam of her lips and she grants me access without hesitation. The trust and acceptance she's always shown me are too much.

She's too much.

My cock strains for space behind the fly of my jeans and I ease my hips back a bit for discretion's sake. For all the foreplay and teasing we've shared, there won't be any true satiation until I claim her innocence and take her as my mate.

Keyla lets off a feminine sound as her body melts against me, her slight frame enveloped by my much larger one. There's no stopping my bear's grumble vibrating up my throat.

This. How could I doubt this is meant to be?

She drops her head back and I draw my tongue down the line of her throat.

Her body goes rigid in my arms.

I pull back. "Did I do something wrong?"

"No." She raises her hand, shielding her gaze from the sun. "What is that?"

Sirens start blaring in the distance as I follow her gaze. Two massive, winged shadows darken the bright, blue sky. They're flying over the newly established portal gate clearing.

The beasts are black and green and— "Holy shit."

"Are they *dragons*?"

My bear roars inside me and I set her onto her feet. "We gotta get back to the clearing."

I shift on the fly and barrel through the forest. A glance to my left assures me Keyla's stunning white wolf is with me.

I might be stronger, but she is faster.

Glancing up, I track the mythical monsters as they extend their scaled wings and circle above the canopy of trees. They cut through the air and then double back toward the clearing, breathing streams of blue fire at the ground below.

I roar, my fury echoing against the trees around us.

Everyone we care about is in that clearing.

My bear is wild as we close the distance, the need to find Brant and protect his mate and cub raging within—

In another racing heartbeat, Calli's phoenix lights up the sky and blocks the dragon's fire. The fiery form of her wildling bird lets off a ball-shriveling scream and sends a stream of orange flame back at them.

Keyla and I break through the treeline and pause to assess what's happening.

Brant, Jaxx, and Kotah are taking down a mutant blue hellhound while Calli bitch-slaps the dragons like you read about.

They don't seem to need backup at the moment.

Keyla shifts back and I follow her lead.

"Where is Mother?" Keyla asks.

I point toward the cabins. "They probably stashed her in— yeah, there. Hawk's got guards on that cabin."

The two of us skirt the edge of the clearing and head toward my construction site. Keyla's attention is solely focused on finding her mother. Mine is on watching her back and protecting her from the chaos still unfolding.

Lukas and Hawk have their guns locked on the shimmering magic of the portal as a fourth invader comes through.

This time, it's a woman.

The mauve-skinned woman struts through the energy of the portal rift and takes in the beat-down in progress. She stands tall and gaunt and has the nerve to look offended. "Stop this! How dare you attack us."

Keyla and I arrive at the framed cabin and the guards open the door and step aside to allow her entry. She races inside and hugs her mother.

I stop on the front step and turn to stand shoulder-to-shoulder with Hawk's men.

Kotah has shifted from his wolf to stand with Hawk as the welcoming committee. I consider jumping in to help Brant with the blue beast, but he and Jaxx are tag-teaming that midnight demon dog and are making their shit look easy.

As they pin the beast to the ground, one of the dragons is thrown to the forest floor and takes out a row of trees. Pixies and fire dervishes scatter and scream.

I check the sky and Calli's got the other dragon in a fiery grasp of her talons and is fighting mid-air. Calli flings the second dragon to the ground. It hits the earth in a staggering thud.

Jaxx and Brant have the beast pinned and are tearing at it with fangs and claws. It's letting off a pitiful bale and I admit, the sound is satisfying.

"Stop! Release my son!"

Hawk stands tall and scowls. "If I stop our defenses, do I have your word the violence ends?"

"You do," the queen says.

He casts a glance toward his mates and the battle ends. The others might not know they can speak over their mating bond but those of us close to the source do.

Jaxx and Brant release their hold and backstep a few feet while Calli lands and downgrades to her woman aflame form.

I shift back and flash on my clothes, staring out at the clusterfuck of first contact. "And a good time was had by all."

CHAPTER THREE

Keyla

"What's going on out there?" I ask Doc as he steps in to join us. "It got quiet all of a sudden."

"The battle is won. A regal-looking woman in a party dress came through and is claiming to be the queen of the other realm. Her son, Creed, and the two dragons got their asses—"

"Language," Mother snaps.

"Apologies, Majesty. The attackers got their pride kicked and are standing down. Hawk and Kotah are talking to her now and trying to calm her down."

"Calm *her* down. Whatever for?" Mother asks.

"She's playing the victim. According to her, her envoys came through the gate in good faith and were set upon by us in brutal force."

Mother frowns and lifts her chin. "If the hostilities have ended, I will join the discussions. Your brother may be the Prime, but I have decades of experience to offer in a situation such as this."

"Of course, you do, Mother." I glance at Raven standing

inside the door. "Will you and the guards outside please escort her?"

"Yes, Majesty."

As they set off, I follow until I get to the threshold. The clearing has erupted in a buzz of bodies and an influx of people standing around waiting to see and hear what's going on.

I lean against the doorframe and exhale.

"I vote we grab a blanket and disappear into the forest for a few hours. Maybe by dinner, they'll have things sorted out and we can get caught up."

"Don't you want to back up Kotah?"

I shake my head. "He's got Hawk, Mother, and his mates to help him. If they needed more hands to fight, I'd jump in, but he's finding his way politically and doesn't need an entourage watching over his shoulder."

"Do you trust your mother to play nice?"

I think about that and watch her standing tall next to my brother. "I do. Political power struggles are her strong suit. She may doubt Kotah privately, but she'll never let anyone else question the Northwood rule. She'll be in her glory helping him fortify against a visiting queen."

Doc waggles his brow and winks. "Well then, I believe you mentioned grabbing a blanket and getting gone. One of the perks of being the head of a construction site is that I have access to the supply crates. Two blankets coming right up."

I grin and flutter my eyelashes at him. "My hero."

Doc leads us into the forest and the further we get from the chaos of the clearing the better this idea feels. We walk upriver for about twenty minutes before we decide to look around and pick a spot.

Part of me feels guilty for abandoning the clearing when so

much is going on, but the other part of me feels like there are so many people involved already we won't be missed.

I text Calli. *If we're needed back, call me. Our four-legged selves can get back in minutes.*

The response comes back almost instantly. *Don't worry. Kotah is handling things. Have fun. Don't do anything I wouldn't do.*

I laugh at the absurdity of that. *Is there anything you wouldn't do?*

Nope. So, enjoy.

I laugh and tuck my phone into my pocket. One of the best parts of Kotah's quint mating is that I inherited a sister and three more brothers. They are all characters and I adore each one.

"So, back to the topic of our mating," I say, catching a few loose strands of my hair and tucking them behind my ear. "You mentioned a soft bed at my back and some privacy. Et voila, here we are, blankets in hand and secluded in the woods."

He chuckles and lifts our joined fingers to kiss my knuckles. "You've got a one-track mind, Miss Northwood. No. Today is not the day. I want your first time to stand out like a dream. Music. Soft lighting. Sweet and sinful snacks. I've got big plans."

It figures. I want him to throw me down and claim me as his own and he wants flowers and romance. "As lovely as that sounds, I don't need it. All I need is you."

He grins, his ebony brow arching as he smiles down at me. "You have me."

"But not all of you."

He chuckles and points to a mossy spot between two massive trees. Handing me one of the blankets, he shakes out the other and spreads it out on the ground. When that's done, he takes the other blanket and tosses it down. "You have all of me. It's me that hasn't had all of you and that's okay. We'll get there."

He laughs at my pouty lip and gives me a quick kiss. Then he reaches behind his shoulders and pulls his shirt over his head. "Let's take a dip in the river. By the time we get back, we'll be ready to have some fun in the sun and warm up in our blankets."

I like the sound of that.

The two of us make quick work of our clothes and I fold them and set them on a rock by the trunk of one of the trees. The autumn air is crisp but thankfully the sun is shining, and wildlings have built-in furnaces.

"Milady." Doc eases down the side of the riverbank and holds his hand out to me.

I giggle. "Do you think my footing is so tenuous that I would fall without the help of a male?"

"I'm hoping for it, actually. I'd like nothing more than to catch you. A tangle of slick and bare body parts sounds good to me."

I laugh and wade deeper into the river.

The chill of the water on my legs is bad but when it inches up the skin of my ribs, goosebumps break loose and I shiver.

Doc's wanton gaze drops straight to the tightening tips of my nipples. "Hello, ladies." He steps deeper into the river and lowers himself until he's eye-level with my breasts. "I missed you. Did you have a good day?"

"They were having a lovely and warm day until my crazy boyfriend talked me into skinny dipping in icy waters."

"Let me warm them up." Pushing forward, he collects me in his arms and claims my breast with his mouth. His kiss is hot and soothing, a stark contrast to the autumn temperature.

I shiver in his arms and he tightens the grip against my back. The languid sweep of lips, tongue, and teeth over the sensitive peak of my nipple brings a rush of warmth to my core.

I groan and push against his ministrations.

"That's my girl," he whispers as he shifts to the other breast. "So responsive. So hungry."

"Yes, hungry. So, why starve me? Take from me what is freely given."

"I will. Don't doubt that. You are mine, Nakeyla Northwood and I am yours."

I reach beneath the moving surface of the river and find the swollen bundle of nerve endings at the crux of my legs. When we got together three months ago, I would never have been so brazen as to touch myself or him so freely.

Since then, we've had many conversations about what he likes and me feeling comfortable with both my body and his is one of those things.

Widening my stance, I drop my head back as he grazes my flesh with his teeth. The gentle scoring raises goosebumps across my skin and I close my eyes.

Being with him is an incredible assault of sensations. It doesn't matter if we're inside or out, warm or cold, standing or on a bed.

As Calli would say, 'S'all good.'

I lace the fingers of my free hand into his hair and crush myself against him. Rubbing my clit lights off a sensual clench and throb of my inner muscles.

They want something substantial to grip. Bent as he is, Dillan's erection is pressed hard against my thigh. The thought of having him penetrating me, of filling me to the limit of my pussy...

"Gods, I want your cock inside me, Dillan Baskins. Enough is enough. Claim me."

He chuckles against my chest and his bear lets off a rumble of approval. "Such language, Princess. What if someone hears you talking like that?"

"If someone is close enough to hear me say I want your cock, the bigger scandal would be what they see."

"Then let's make it worth a scandal."

"Yes. Let's."

I shut out the world and focus on the sensations bombarding me. His mouth is so hot against my skin... my fingers pressing and rubbing... the cool water splashing up my side as we shift and sway.

I close my eyes and fight the cresting of my orgasm.

Not yet.

The tension of my release is grabbing hold of my insides. It ebbs. It wants to break free. My wolf lets off a growl of pleasure and my willpower breaks.

I gasp as the grip of detonation takes me over and my body quakes with the pulse of pleasure unleashed.

Yes, this.

But standing in a river and using my fingers isn't what I want. The orgasm ebbs away too soon and leaves me hungry for so much more. "Please. I want to feel you thrusting inside me. I *need* to be filled by this."

I grip his cock and step closer.

He chuckles as he lifts me from the water and carries me back to our pallet in the trees. For a moment I think I've worn him down and won the battle.

He merely lays me on my back and moves down the little mattress to kneel between my legs.

"Open your knees for me, babe."

I recognize the rasp in his voice and my body responds. The shameless obedience of my legs is embarrassing. It's as if all they want to do is fall open for him.

They do.

If it were anyone else but him, I'd be mortified. But hey, don't judge the Prime Princess by her cover.

Doc's bear lets off a throaty growl. "Look at how your pussy glistens in the sunlight, princess. So beautiful. Let's see if it tastes as good as it looks."

When he drops down and takes me with his mouth, my body explodes with wanton.

I am nothing but desire. Hunger. Need.

I gasp, squirming against his tongue. "More of that."

He wraps his arms around my hips and forces my legs open wider to make space for his broad shoulders.

I giggle as my leg muscles stretch. "By all means, make yourself at home."

Doc

I do. With my mouth fused to her core, I nip and play, showing her how delicious she is. Show don't tell, right? She's fucking ambrosia and eating her fuels me. Yes, it's agony to not be inside her but I meant what I said. I couldn't live with myself if we mated too soon and she regretted rushing into things.

Besides, this is almost as good.

Almost.

She tastes like sweet passion and when I key her up just right, her wolf howls for more. My lips skim over her mound, my tongue flicking and swirling, teasing her engorged clit.

She moans into my mouth, tangling her fingers into my hair and arching into my touch. "I want more."

Yeah, she does.

My little princess is a greedy little minx.

I'm thick and hard and stretch out on the blanket to grind my hips. The friction of fabric rubbing against my cock isn't the same as getting squeezed by her greedy core but it keeps me from doing something stupid like penetrating her out of pure lust.

There will never be enough orgasms to sate my need for her but if I'm lucky, I can appease my cock.

I growl, rubbing my face in her juices, slicking my lips so her feminine scent covers my mouth. Fuck she tastes good.

Her legs quiver and her breath quickens.

She won't last long.

That's good because I'm going to cream this blanket and I don't want to go off before her. With urgency more than finesse, I swipe my fingers through the moist heat of her folds and then tease and tickle at her entrance.

Keyla wants more, so I'll give her more.

She meant my cock, but fingers will have to do. I've been damned careful the few times I've penetrated her like this, which is tough because the moment I start massaging her, she practically impales herself.

I'm ready for it, though, and I'm in control of the depth and pressure. As I expect, the moment I finger her, she bucks for more. Her unbridled response sends a shot of hot pleasure straight into my cock.

Fuck. I need inside her so bad it's killing me.

I groan, pumping my cock against the mattress like a teenager in need of a free hand. "Come for me, babe. Right into my mouth. Feed your male."

Her energy surges as a throaty cry cuts the air. I focus on her breathy gasps as long as I can, riding out her pleasure before my hard-on demands a moment.

When she's crested and is sinking into her afterglow, I grind my hips down, thrusting on the flimsy blanket. My breath catches and I don't last long.

Hot cum streams free as my shoulders lock and my abs convulse. I try not to make it too dramatic because the more I draw attention to my release, the more she pressures me to fuck her.

My restraint is at its end.

Yes, wildlings have sex without claiming their partners and binding one another for life, but I know I won't have that much control.

She. Is. Mine.

As the two of us pant for air, I climb forward and flop on the blanket next to her. Reaching to the side, I pull the other blanket over us to keep her from getting chilled as much as to offer her a bit of privacy.

"Hello, beautiful." I kiss the tattooed choker on her neck and draw my tongue over the intertwining vines and detailed fretwork. It's a symbol of wildling royalty.

Her brother has one too.

The design is penned in a rich wine with blacks, browns, and greens. The ink has magical fae properties that glisten in any light. And over the center of her throat sits the royal Northwood crest with a wolf's head tipped back and howling at a full moon.

I run a gentle caress from the wolf's nose, along her collarbone, and over the soft round of her shoulder. "Nice afternoon for a dip, wasn't it?"

She giggles and rolls closer. "I think so."

CHAPTER FOUR

Creed

Kill me. Someone put me out of my fucking misery. A couple of hours ago we were instructed to burst through the gate and show the fae of this realm what we are made of. Ha. The tides were turned. Spectacularly.

The bitch queen is so conceited it's unbelievable.

With her dirty little alliance with a resident realm outlaw, she thought she had her expansion plans locked down? Idiotic. If she spent even a tenth of the time listening to and learning from great leaders like I did, she would have seen what a misstep that was.

Cue me being pinned to the forest floor and seething with fury. Once again I'm overpowered and left looking like a failure.

Life sucks when you're living with your hands tied behind your back… or your powers locked away.

If she wanted me to be her little prince taking point in her battles, she should've left me as I was. I was far more deadly as a faery warrior who could attack the minds of my enemy than I am as a possessed blue beast.

Not that I'll ever be that man again.

Between having my wings hacked off and being cursed by Laryssa's blood witch, I'll never again be the man I once was.

Boohoo, such a sad, sad story.

"So, dragons, eh? And twins, that's cool."

I chuckle to myself as Calli tries to make nice with the Silverwing twins. True, she is the woman behind the phoenix but by my estimation, she's nothing but a street thug blonde with bright green eyes and nice tits.

When she gets nothing but hostility from the dragon douche duo, she turns her charms on me. "And what? You're guardians of the prince here?"

She gestures to me and I pretend she's not totally checking me out. I've been weighed and measured before. Let her form her opinions, I don't give a shit.

She glances from me to the queen, and I can almost hear her comparing me to my 'mother'. *He looks nothing like the queen. His skin isn't mauve and his features are chiseled without being angular. She's gaunt and willowy and doesn't have a fraction of the gentry and presence he's obviously been bred with.*

Okay, I may have taken some personal license with that last bit.

"So, not an overly chatty bunch." She shrugs and takes a seat on the log by the fire. "Yes, we beat the snot out of you, but we can still be friends."

"Sleck off."

Aw, Vik. A gentleman and a scholar.

Calli cracks a smile. "Sweet, they do speak."

The jaguar shifter leans back against his log and crosses his ankles. Jaxx is a long, tall drink of southern charm and after having his teeth and claws tearing at my skin, I admit, he's also one hell of a fighter.

"My suggestion, boys," he says, his drawl thick, "do not piss us off. We're neighbors now. Instead, ask and answer questions. We worked for months to open this rift and honestly, your lack of appreciation is underwhelming."

"You didn't beat us," Vik snipes, glaring at Calli.

She laughs. "Oh, yeah. I totes did. Tomorrow, if you want a rematch, we can try again. Maybe I won't let them use my tears to heal you, though. Maybe a little suffering would humble you up a bit."

If only that were true.

Whatever chip Vik and Rhy have on their shoulders, it holds them hostage. They might be okay guys if they weren't such driven assholes.

Her comment about them suffering a little earns her a couple of impressive scowls from the dragon twins.

Good. It serves them right.

Dragons may be the top of the wildling heap in our realm, but this is a brave new world. I'm looking forward to a little reshuffling of power.

A rise from the ashes if you will.

"So, you are an honest to gods phoenix," Rhy says.

"Yep. And you two are twin dragons. I *do* think that's cool. Do you have cool matchy names or anything?"

"No."

"So, do I get to know your names?"

"No."

"Alrighty then. Good talk."

I've seen this show before and it's boring. The dragon twins take egotistical posturing to new levels. I don't know if it's a dragon thing or a 'they're dicks' thing. Either way, I don't feel like playing today.

"Their names are Vikarus and Rhylan, or Vik and Rhy to their friends."

"Which you're not," Vik snaps.

"Understood, dragon boy," the phoenix says holding up her hands.

Rhylan glares at me. What's the matter, dragon? Did I ruin your air of dark and broody mystery? It's your name, asshole. Everything is a power struggle with them.

"So," Calli says, taking another run at them, "the realm you're from. Is it all fae and magical creatures?"

What an odd question.

"As opposed to what?" I ask.

She shrugs. "Well, I was born and raised human, and then I transitioned to a wildling and was reborn. I was wondering if the entire population of your realm is fae and magical or if you have... I don't know, non-magicals, or aliens, or sea creatures or something. Help a girl out. I'm trying to start a convo."

This isn't a fireside camp and we're not happy little campers. Hello... cursed prisoner here. No one on our side is looking for new friends.

I sigh. "How about we don't?"

Calli flashes me a look and shrugs. "Fine. Consider that over. Sulk all you want, broody boys. I was trying to be nice."

"No one's nice for no reason," I say.

"Maybe in your world. In this world, most people are nice and the ones who aren't are the exception."

I chuff. What world are you living in, female... Oh, right. This one.

Keyla

After a couple of lazy and sexy hours with Doc, dusk encroaches on the light of day and the temperature begins to drop. Wrapped in his arms and covered by a blanket, I could

43

comfortably stay here all night. I can't, however, take the growling of his stomach any longer.

"Ignore it."

I laugh. "Neither of us will sleep if we don't feed the beast. Besides, if I'm going to be Kotah's assistant, I suppose I should show up when realm-altering events are taking place."

"So mature."

"I thought so."

The two of us dress and fold up our blankets before abandoning our private spot along the river. My muscles are tired and a little jittery from the sex but it's the best kind of tired strain. I feel loose-limbed and very relaxed.

"Calli says Kotah, Hawk, and Mother are still off with Queen Laryssa of Dornte. It looks like she, Jaxx, and Brant are hosting a fireside meet and greet with the prince and the dragon twins."

"Oh, yeah?" he chuckles, pausing so I can walk in front of him as we climb through a tight area of brush. "Brant and Jaxx are hanging out with three aggressive strangers and their pregnant mate. I can imagine how well that's going."

I smile. "There is likely a lot of growling."

"Very likely."

I swing our joined hands between us, thinking about that. One thing I've learned from joining them on their quest is that the five of them handle their issues. "It's nice how they gelled as a unit."

"Nice for them, yeah."

I hear the pang of resentment in his words and squeeze his hand. "You'll always be his best friend and his brother from another mother. Him loving his mates adds love for them, it doesn't take any away from you."

"That doesn't mean we don't get left behind in the process. No matter how good they've been about including us, the structure of their lives has changed. They have four more people who now rank higher than us. We have become the tagalongs."

As much as it hurts to hear it, Doc's not wrong.

"And soon that will be five. Once the baby arrives, they'll be even more consumed by their own lives."

"Do phoenixes have one baby like wolves or multiples like bears and lions?" he asks.

"I don't know. I don't suppose anyone knows. We're in uncharted territory here. I guess we'll have to wait and see."

He lets off a heavy sigh and casts me a sidelong glance. "It's the beginning of the end of the lives we had with them. Not that I begrudge them any of it. I think it's amazing and I'm so freaking excited for this baby."

"Oh, I know. I get it. I miss the days of me and Kotah too but am thrilled about the pregnancy."

We grow quiet as we approach the clearing, partly because wildlings and other fae species have incredibly acute hearing and partly because neither of us wants to give up the privacy of our stolen hours.

But then his stomach rumbles again and I laugh. "There's no taming that beast, is there?"

Doc pats his belly and grins. "Only one way. Feed me, female. After a strenuous afternoon, your male needs nourishment."

"I think I fed you well for the past three hours."

The growl that rumbles from his chest is all sass. "Yes, you did, Princess. I am a truly blessed male."

I wave to Calli as we exit the trees and check out the three strangers. The two I can see are obviously the dragon twins and that means the prince is the one with his back to me. He has long, silver hair. "I'm getting a Witcher vibe over there."

Doc chuckles. "Got a thing for Geralt of Rivia, do you, babe?"

"Um... yeah. Henry Cavill is drool-worthy. I would not kick him out of my bed."

He laughs. "You wouldn't have to. If Henry Cavill was in your bed, I'd join the two of you."

That fills me with all kinds of warm and fuzzy.

I chuckle and cast another glance toward the fireside crew. The dragons are broadly built and wear a long shaggy mane of blond hair that hangs over their eyes. So much so, I can't say for sure they have eyes.

"What the fiery karnos is that?" One of the twins says, pointing at the sky.

I follow his gesture to see what he's referring to and watch the silver jet trail an exhaust cloud across the dusky mauve-gray sky above.

"It's an airplane," Calli says. "It's a vehicle to travel long journeys through the air."

The twins laugh. "That's what wings are for."

I chuckle. To them, I suppose that's true.

"Yes," Calli says, "but here in the human realm, only birds, bats, and airplanes have wings. There are no such things as dragons or phoenixes or pixies in this realm. We live secretly among the humans and can't have you two soaring through the sky."

"A great reason to go home," a dragon says.

"But you just got here."

"You have a touch of asshole in you, you know that?" The graveled baritone of the male's voice has me focusing on the conversation.

"Thanks. I work at it." Calli winks and casts the prince a smartass smile.

"Come to papa," Doc says, heading straight over to the food table.

I'm stuck in place. The prince's voice is deep and has a cadence and an accent to it that is sexy as hell. I want him to speak again. I crave it, actually.

Damn. Why are my fingers tingling?

"What about food?" he asks. "Do prisoners get to eat in this realm?"

Calli gestures toward us and grins. "You're not our prisoners. We're just shooting the shit. If you want food, help yourself. But understand, if you try anything, we're ready and very willing to kick your asses."

The man's entire frame tenses. "Watch yourself, phoenix. You might have bested us in your full, warrior form, but as a female, you're weak and vulnerable to any number of attacks."

Doc and I both growl and turn to focus on the threat made. Not that we need to. Brant and Jaxx are both on their feet and creating a screen in front of their female.

Creed stands and lifts his palms. "I take it by how much the brute here has eaten that it's not poisoned?"

Brant flashes him his teeth, and points for him to move off. "No. If we wanted you dead, you'd be dead."

Prince Creed takes the hint and vacates the fire circle to head over to the catering table. He's tall and walks with a level of grace uncommon in a man of his size.

As he eyes up the selection on the food table, Doc and I step back to give him the first run at things.

"Did you guys really cut off the head of the other guy's father?" he asks. His back to us as he amasses a plate of food Doc seems impressed with.

"It happened," Calli says, obviously not willing to get into it. She grabs a paper plate and grabs a couple of egg rolls. "Did your mother really think she could send you three in and overtake our realm?"

"She's not my mother." The brusque finality of that holds unmistakable violence.

"Easy." Jaxx steps between Calli and Creed, his hands raised. My sweet, Texan brother-in-law may have a wicked sense of humor and a warm smile but he's also wildly protective of his mates. And now that Calli's pregnant... multiply that by a million. "Down, boy."

The dragon twins are on their feet and rushing forward to back up their prince. Doc and I shift position to cover Calli if trouble is brewing.

The food table is suddenly a very crowded place.

It's a regular inter-realm, wildling standoff.

Creed must sense our movement behind him because he turns around and—

Our gaze locks.

Energy jolts through my body and lights up my cells. His eyes, fully black, flip to opal as something brutal and invasive passes between us.

My heart burns inside my chest.

I can't breathe.

Light explodes inside my mind and luminescent shrapnel short-circuits my cognitive function. One moment my world is lit up—the next, everything goes dark.

I crumple and fall to the forest floor.

Doc

"What the fuck?" I drop to my knees to examine Keyla as she collapses to the ground. It's a blessing that my medical experience kicks in during moments like this because the man and the bear are losing their shit.

"What did you do to him," one of the twins shouts.

"Nothing," Calli says. "I didn't instigate simultaneous fainting." She kneels on the ground beside me checking on Keyla while Jaxx checks the status of the silver-haired prince.

"Well then, what happened?" one of them asks while the other one checks over his shoulder.

"Creed, wake up. If she comes back and sees you like this, we're all dead. Come on. Get up."

I'm not sure what the hell that means but I don't care. Whatever hit them seems to be over. Keyla and Creed wake at the same moment.

Like—*exactly*—the same moment.

It's freaky and I don't like it. The two of them stir from their dirt nap and then snap awake.

"Are you okay, girlfriend?" Calli asks, stroking Keyla's hair away from her face.

Tears pool in her eyes as she stands. The silver-headed prince matches her stance and looks almost as upset. He's staring at her and my bear doesn't like the intensity of the gaze one bit.

Keyla seems oblivious to him as she turns to look at the portal gate. "I'm sorry," she says, her tears falling in a steady stream. She meets my gaze and there's a depth of confusion and sadness there I don't understand. "I'm sorry."

Before I can ask her what the hell is going on, she launches into the air, bursting into her wolf. Creed does the same and explodes into that massive midnight blue nightmare.

The two of them bolt off and my head spins.

What the actual fuck is happening?

Jaxx, Doc, and Brant shout and burst into the chase, but despite their objections, Keyla's wolf and that demon dog dive at the rift.

My heart collapses when they pass right through the pulsing energy and land in the clearing. I catch up to Jaxx and the others and they look as confused as I do.

"What happened?" Calli asks, looking bewildered. "Why are they still here?"

Lukas steps into the mix looking pissed. "I shut the bridge down. We already have one hostile queen, two dragons, and a demon shifter. I figured that's enough surprises for one day."

"You're the man, Lukas." Jaxx holds up his palms toward the two wolves snarling at us. "Any ideas on what we do about them?"

Lukas shakes his head. "None."

"There's nothing you can do," a man in an FCO uniform says. Brant introduced us yesterday... Mallory, I think his name is. He's the hulderfolk security guard from Manhattan who Hawk asked to oversee the gate. "Those two are soul seared."

"What the fuck does that mean, little man," I snap. "What did he do to her?"

I give the guy credit. I've barely got a hold on my bear and he doesn't look the least bit worried. "He did nothing. It's something that happens. Two souls mirrored so perfectly that when they stand face to face, they are bound for life. It's irreversible."

I swallow as the spinning in my head amps up to a full centrifuge. Hulderfolk can't lie, but how can this be true? Keyla doesn't even know him.

"They're strangers," Calli says, matching my thoughts. "... and from different realms... and Keyla and Doc are together..."

Damn straight we are.

All eyes land on me and the pity and devastation in those gazes spear me through the heart.

"We'll figure this out," Calli says. "Mallory, maybe you're mistaken. How can you be so sure this is a soul searing thing?"

"Because *I'm* soul seared." He offers me a sympathetic smile and extends his palm out to me. "You'll see. When they shift back, they'll wear a mating mark. It's quite wonderful. Something to celebrate."

I lock my gaze on the tattoo marking the flesh of his palm and my bear weighs in on that. A murderous growl tears from my throat. I lose my hold on my shift and drop to all fours baring my teeth.

Calli sighs and looks to her mates for help. "Maybe we should hold off on the champagne for a bit."

CHAPTER FIVE

Creed

*F*ate is a fucking asshole. First, my family lands are invaded and the bitch Laryssa of Nowhere activates traitorous sleeper agents within the palace. Then, my family is destroyed, my powers are locked, and I'm cursed into servitude as a demon dog monster. Now I get dragged to this land of narys and weaklings to be *soul seared* to a fucking female?

A *female!*

That is wrong on so many levels.

Still, the agony in her dark chocolate eyes gives me some comfort. It's not only me who suffers. She doesn't want this either. She has her heart set on another.

The black bear shifter they call Doc.

The beast snarls, saliva dripping to the trampled ground surrounding the portal gate. The only thing keeping me from ripping his throat out is the fact that the two of them never mated.

They wear each other on their flesh but it's only by contact. They aren't mates.

Sorry, loser. Soul seared trumps love.

Soul seared trumps everything.

The phenomenon of mating this way is the thing of legends. Two souls mirrored so perfectly that when they bond, they are bound for life. It's the stuff of bedtime stories—an impossible myth.

Yeah, kinda like a Fae Phoenix resurrecting from the dead to open the rift between the two realms.

The day is full of surprises.

When the bear moves closer, I hunch low to the ground and snarl. *Back off, cockwad.*

She is *mine.*

I have no idea how that works yet but there is no way another male who has intimate knowledge of my female will take what's mine.

Too much has been taken from me already.

Teeth bared, muscles tensed, and ready to attack, I make it clear if that black furball tries to advance, I will rip him to shreds.

"Okay, enough," Jaxx snaps. His alpha command rings in the air as he steps between us. "Brant, you take Doc somewhere and get him calmed down. Creed, I need you to stand the fuck down, my man. Yes, this is a clusterfuck of monumental proportion, but a territorial bloodbath over Keyla won't help."

"What about one of the cabins?" the phoenix says, pointing toward the area under construction. "The two of them can be alone and calm down."

"Good idea, kitten. Creed and Keyla, how about a little privacy to figure things out? Let's head over to the temporary housing and take a moment to breathe."

Breathe? I can't breathe. I'm vibrating with a bombardment of impulses.

I need to get back to my side of the gate.

I need to slaughter anyone who gets in my way.

I need to calm my female and make things right.

I need them to open the gate and let us follow the beacon that calls to us. I glare at the shimmering energy.

The call of our mating demands we return. I glance at the energy fluctuation of the rift again and growl.

"Sorry, guys," Jaxx says. "No one is goin' anywhere until we know more. It's the cabin for some privacy or nothin'."

Not good enough. We need to get through the gate and away from here. I bare my teeth and hold my ground. There's no way I'm volunteering to be locked in a wooden box. It sounds an awful lot like a coffin.

I've been shackled and held prisoner for the past two years. I open my maw and let out a violent roar.

Jaxx backs Calli away but makes no move to let us go. My little wolf whines beside me but there's nothing I can do about that right now. I've got her flank and am watching the sight-lines. I'll keep her safe until we figure out how to get back to Dornte.

You're safe, Little Wolf. I will keep you safe.

There's likely only one person in this camp who poses any danger to her—the bitch queen Laryssa.

There's no way that woman will hurt my wolf mate. She killed my last love. I won't let her kill this one too.

Keyla

My body aches as I finally lower myself onto the plywood floor of one of the temporary cabins. The call of magic pulling at me is relentless and painful but Kotah and Hawk don't seem to understand our need to leave. After an hour of growling and whining, I am too exhausted to try any longer.

If I could only shift back and talk to them.

Somehow, the soul searing has trapped us in our animal form. It's frightening and frustrating to be prevented from taking my other form but no matter how hard I try to calm down and focus on shifting, I remain a wolf.

Maybe by morning, I'll have more control.

I rest my muzzle on my front paws and try to shut out the world. Closing my eyes, I wish this soul searing nightmare was only that—a nightmare.

When I open my eyes, I want to wake from this bad dream in the warmth of Doc's arms. I envision him lying beside me, rolling my hair through his fingers, and watching me sleep like usual.

With anxiety pressing on my chest, I draw a deep breath and open my eyes. Doc's hazel green gaze isn't what I find. I'm staring into two swirling white opal pools glittering with gold.

There are no pupils. They are solid eerie globes. The soft whine that escapes my throat isn't intentional.

I am sorry, Little Wolf, he says into my mind. *I'm not much to look at in this form. We both know you deserve better than to be paired with me. The fae universe crossed its streams of magic matchmaking somewhere and we are left to pay the price.*

The words land in my mind and my gaze darts frantically to figure out where it's coming from. He's in my head? Kotah and his mates can communicate over a mental channel, but they're mates...

Are you alright?

No. I don't understand any of this. I've never heard of soul searing. Are we sure that is what this is?

I'm sure. Somehow the unseen forces decided we should be bonded evermore.

Evermore?

You're certain it's permanent? My heart swells in the beat of silence between my words and his answer. Maybe there's a chance it can be reversed. Maybe there's a chance I can be with Doc—

Yes. It is permanent.

I close my eyes, my burgeoning hope crushed with those two simple words. How can the universe think I should be with this man when my heart beats for another? I've lived the past three months watching this same scenario unfold in my brother's life but this isn't like what happened to Kotah.

He was unattached and honored to be paired as Calli's mate. I chose my path. It led me to Doc.

Please don't cry.

I wipe my muzzle against my paw and draw a labored breath. *I'm overwhelmed. I'm trying. There's just too much happening. It all hurts.*

He tilts his head to the side and lowers himself onto the floor beside me. When our gazes meet on the same level, he shifts his much larger paw to touch mine. *Then let's slow it down. My name is Creed Thornebane, Prince of Dornte. I am a mind guardian, and my realm has been overthrown by a spiteful purple bitch.*

I take that in and nod. *My name is Nakeyla Northwood, Prime Princess of the Human Realm. I am a wolf wildling, and my brother is our king. He is the strongest, most honorable male I have ever known.*

He tilts his head and straightens. *I didn't realize you were a princess. That makes more sense.*

Does it? Why?

Because perhaps we weren't paired to be bound as lovers. We are both royals in a position to influence the coming change now that a bridge has been established between our realms. Perhaps we're meant to unite the two realms and lead the way to a new order.

I consider that and brighten. *That makes more sense to me than us being mates... no offense meant.*

Me too... and none taken.

If we truly share mirrored souls, I owe it to him to address things as I would like them to be addressed if roles were reversed. *I don't mean to be rude, but if we're being honest, Dillan Baskins, the very upset black bear you met a moment ago... is my male. He claimed my heart and we plan to mate.*

His beast swells in size and lets off a terrifying sound. It vibrates in my chest and quickens my breath. My wolf shies away from the territorial reaction to my statement. I've lived my entire life with Alpha males, so I understand it, but that doesn't mean I like it.

I know this is a difficult situation, but you and I just met. How can you be upset about the feelings I have for a male I am already involved with?

He closes his eyes and after a few long breaths, he opens them and seems much calmer. *It's the magic of the searing. I have little control over it and it has nothing to do with logic... or me. You are mine, Nakeyla. I will die to protect that bond.*

So quickly? I don't believe it.

Then let me tell you about the woman of my heart, Little Wolf. Her name is Bloom and she is an earth guardian. She is tall and her skin tastes like sunshine, while her hair smells like the sweetest summer blossoms.

The growl that rends the air is nothing I can control.

You don't appreciate hearing about the woman who moans her pleasures for me at night?

His words twist deep in my belly and incite the rage of my wolf. My instinct to snap and tear her flesh from bone rise within me like a tsunami of hostile emotion.

Picturing him loving another hits a nerve.

Why should it matter? It makes no sense, but it *does* matter. I'm not sure what kind of violence he sees in me, but whatever my reaction, it's more magic than me.

I cut off my wolf's protest and focus on him. *How can I want to kill a woman I don't even know over a man I just met? It makes no sense.*

He cants his head to one side. He is neither wolf nor dog.

I've never seen any creature like him. Then again, I've never seen dragons before either until this morning.

I am sorry the universe disregarded your plans with the bear. For his safety, you should likely not tell me how much you love him. I won't mean to harm him, but the beast and I aren't friends and sometimes I lose control.

If *my* reaction is any indication of the kind of violence my declarations would unleash on Doc, I agree. I don't want to set his demon dog on him either.

Alright, I'll try not to bring him up if you'll do me the same courtesy. No more Bloom stories. I'd hate to kill someone as my first act in your realm.

The musical tenor of his laughter triggers something sinful within me. It's disarming, endearing, completely sexual. It coils within me like liquid heat and warms parts of me a stranger shouldn't be warming.

I swallow as the sound of his amusement zings a keening heat to my nipples and then my clenching core. This isn't real. Whatever is happening is someone else's plan, not mine.

I love Doc. I want Doc.

I'm sorry. I'm not sure if I'm saying that to Doc or Creed, but it works for either.

You have nothing to apologize for.

Ha! You don't know what's going through my body and mind right now. I definitely need to apologize.

Again, he floods my mind with the warm caress of his male amusement. *I promise you, I don't hold you responsible for any inappropriate hungers. We are both being bombarded by the need to unite.*

So, it's not just me?

Most certainly not. Trust me. This will go better for both of us if we remain civil and understanding of one another. This happened to both of us. Neither wants it. Neither can do anything about it. As long as I'm in control, nothing will happen between us that we don't want. I'm not that kind of male.

And what if you're not in control?

Let's focus on not letting that happen.

Great idea. I let out a long breath and try to focus on convincing my wolf to stand down. *I understand we don't have to be enemies, but my wolf wants to fight.*

Mine too—except fighting each other does neither of us any good. For better or worse, it's the two of us now and there is nothing to be done about it.

I wince. I hate to hear him say that, but something inside me knows he's right. *So, what now?*

I have a few ideas. We must convince your brother to allow us through the gate so we can find the source of this pull burning inside us.

I prop up onto my elbows and search his gaze. *That sounds good. Whatever the universe has in mind, we aren't the navigators of our stars. There's something important that needs to be addressed.*

Agreed. He dips his head and nuzzles the fur of my neck. The touch is gentle and polite but triggers another zing of sensations I shouldn't feel for him.

But it doesn't matter.

It's not real.

∼

Doc

I storm through the shadows of the trees while my bear burns off some of his urge to kill. Darkness has fallen and if it weren't for night vision, there would be no maneuvering in the dense forest at all.

I had it.

For one brief moment, I had my world as I wanted it. I had a beautiful, sweet, intelligent girl who loved me and who I would die for.

I took the high road to be the man I wanted to be.

Ironic. The old me, would've sweet-talked Keyla out of her clothes and mated her months ago. I didn't want to do that. Not only is she young, but she's been sheltered as the fucking Prime Princess her whole life.

I wanted to go slow, to get Kotah's blessing, to be the gentleman she deserves.

I rear up on my back paws and press my massive palms against a leaning tree. My claws catch the moonlight as it pushes its way through the canopy. With all of my bear's strength, I pump my muscles and push and bounce and push again until the crack of lumber brings the oversized toothpick crashing to the forest floor.

And what the fuck was that part about running for the gate? Screw you, Doc, I'm eloping with the blue demon dog. After everything we've done together, both as part of the Guardian team and behind closed doors, I don't even rank a Dear John moment?

My bear lets off another thundering roar.

Fuck this. If this is what love does to a person, I was better off being a good time guy and not caring.

I glance down at the thick black fur covering my muscled chest. Is my heart still beating behind the slotted screen of my ribcage? I can't see how. It feels like it's been ripped out and left nothing but a gaping hole for the cold wind to blow through.

Figures. The universe steps in for Brant and he gets four perfect soul mates.

The universe steps in for me and I get left behind.

Story of my fucking life.

Hell, one minute you're the man of her dreams and the next you're uprooting trees and making a damned fool of yourself while your female hunkers down with another man.

I lean back and roar at the night sky.

I should've mated her while I had the chance.

With all the hot and heavy vibes going on between us, I could've claimed her, and then she'd have *my* mating mark all over her.

She doesn't.

And now she's with *him*.

"My brother," Brant says, tracking my movements as I rage. "I'm here for you. Shift back and tell me what I can do?"

I roar and flash him my teeth.

If I knew a guy's life had been obliterated, I would read the fact that he lost his shit and take it as a sign he needs some fucking space.

Not Brant.

Brant is a well-meaning oaf most times, but he has the courage of a warrior and the heart of a teddy bear. And he's a grizzly, so there's no time in life when he's not bigger or stronger than me... which is a piss-off actually, since I'm older.

He also never gives up. Never.

The only way I'll gain any peace is to shift back and let him have his say. I growl and force my bear to recede so I can get things done.

The moment I stand on two feet and flash some clothes on, he pulls me against his broad chest for a bone-crushing bear hug.

"How are you, my brother?"

I fight the string of nasty responses firing in my head. How can he ask such a stupid, fucking question while the combined scents of his mates and sex waft off his skin like an overdone body spray?

"How do you think I am?" I push back from his massive frame. If he's going to start doling out relationship advice after scrambling like a horny idiot for the past three months, I'll pound him.

I will literally, flat out, punch him in his face.

"How would you be if you were in my shoes?"

Brant holds up his hands. His dark, chestnut waves rustle against his muscled shoulders as his gaze narrows. "Hello? The universe stepped in and smacked me in the balls with a mating bond, remember?"

"But you were the one *included* in the mating bond, not the one left out in the cold."

He lifts his shoulder. "I'll give you that."

"Gee, thanks."

The low rumble of his growl doesn't intimidate me. His grizzly has always been standoffish. "You won't improve your situation by shitting on everyone around you. How about you pull up your Calvins and calm the fuck down."

"How about you go back to the cabin I built you, go another round with your soul mates, and then come back and look at where I am. Don't compare us, B. We're not in the same boat here."

He shrugs those broad shoulders and tosses up his hands. "Got it. Look, I get that you just got fucked over by the universe but the dust hasn't even settled. Kotah will speak to them. Maybe if you're done being a miserable prick, you could tag along and join the convo."

Join the convo?

"And what, exactly do you think I gain from joining that particular convo? The moment their bonding hit—"

"It was a searing technically—Mine was a bonding, they are soul seared—sorry, go on."

Such an annoying asshole. "The moment their *searing* hit, she looked at me, said she was sorry, and tried to run off with the guy. I think that says a lot about where this is headed."

"Maybe," Calli says, tromping through the scrub to join us.

A mumbled curse escapes under my breath, followed by a warning growl from Brant's bear. I send him an apologetic glance and try to rein it in.

Brant's mate is a busty blonde with a sarcastic wit and a fiery bite. He seriously won the lottery when it comes to the attractiveness of his four mates.

It sucks for Keyla that her mate is part demon freak.

Calli stops before me and pulls me in for a hug. The woman was raised human and doesn't understand the personal space of a wildling.

She's a hugger.

"Maybe you're right and Keyla wanted to run with him, or maybe she was overwhelmed and made a bad call in a heated moment. It happens."

Brant wraps his arm around his mate and leans down the foot and a half to kiss the top of her head. "But shit like that can be fixed. Don't close the door, is all I'm saying. If I'd given up when Calli said it was hopeless and ran away, we wouldn't be where we are now."

I stare at the two of them and my chest tightens to the point I can't breathe. Where the five of them are right now is pretty great. A full five-way love bond, everyone included, and now a baby on the way. "I want to believe that, you know I do, but I don't see how—"

Calli holds up her finger and cuts me off. "Love conquers all is a time-tested saying for a reason, Doc."

"Hells yeah, it is, beautiful."

She smiles up at Brant and then turns that loving glow on me. "It's too soon to consider yourself defeated, Bear. Put a little faith in Keyla. If her mating is anything like mine, she's reeling. She needs a moment to sort through what the universe threw at her. Hang in there."

When she's done, Calli holds up her hands in surrender. "Sermon over. I need to eat again before I go to bed or I'll get hangry. Remember what I said. They are just as angry and in shock as you are."

I want to believe she's right.

It feels like too much of a risk.

Brant wraps his tree-trunk of an arm around my neck and headlocks me like when we were cubs. "Come on, Dilly bear. Calli's right. You need to have a little faith in Keyla."

I plow my fist into the tender flesh of his kidneys. He buckles forward and releases me from his hold.

"You're an ass, Brant."

"True story. Smartass. Pain in the ass. Nice piece of ass. Yeah, it's a burden."

I roll my eyes. "Fine. Where's your wolf? Maybe he can help me get some answers."

CHAPTER SIX

Creed

*A*fter our talk, Keyla seems calmer and I'm pretty sure I've done at least one thing right. Letting her see my anger and denying our bond will only torture us both. There is no strategic advantage to take that stand. If she's been sent as an ally in my fight against Laryssa, being a dick won't help me, my family, or our people.

Perhaps this searing *is* a strategic alliance to unite the two realms. That I can wrap my head around.

And while normally, soul seared shifters of any species can't reclaim their human forms for days or weeks, I'm not normal—understatement of the century.

My psychogenesis has been tethered since Laryssa invaded, but something about the magic of the searing, or my connection with Keyla jarred things loose.

We spoke over my mental channel.

I haven't been able to do that in over two years.

If I have access to that, maybe I have access to some of my other gifts as well.

Sitting in the center of the wooden floor, I close my eyes and focus on the arcane power of my ancestors.

There is much to do, and it will be easier as a man.

As my heritage power builds in my cells, Laryssa's curse attacks. The crippling pain is meant to keep me pinned within the confines of her prison. It's excruciating. It feels like someone is scraping a heated blade across my internal organs. I lock my shoulders and brace my weight against my paws, growling as my nature wars with what I've been forced to become.

Keyla whines beside me and I curse again.

Is our pain connected? I didn't think of that.

I'm sorry. This will be over soon. Bear it with me and then we will be in a better position.

The blood curse binding me is as much mental as it is physical, so I let my mind recede, distancing me from the haunting devastation I'm infected with each time I fight the queen's tethers.

I sense Keyla's horror.

This is how she tries to control me. It's over now. Put it out of your head.

It's... horrible.

It is. I've seen the images a thousand times. My father having his throat ripped out, my mother stripped naked and thrown down the stone staircase in front of our castle, my sister captured and beaten against the polished floor of the courtyard.

It's barbaric.

It's over. The past cannot hurt us unless we let it.

I reinforce my resolve and call forward the power of the ancient crown guardians—the Amberloq warriors. Unsure if my call will be heeded from across the span of realms, or if there are any members of the royal guardians even still alive, I wait...

and focus...

and bear the agony.

The web of connections I used to access without effort is

gone—severed by Laryssa's blood witch and her curse. It's been lonely, being the only one in my mind.

And even though the universe erred in pairing me with a wildling wolf, having access to Keyla's mind is a gift. Mind energy is what fuels me.

I startle as an influx of power tingles in the back of my synapses. It starts as a trickle but grows to a stream and then a tsunami. Somewhere, there are others—the Amberloq are not extinguished.

That, in itself, makes enduring this pain worthwhile.

I've been so isolated, I'd lost hope.

Mind firing, I focus on not blacking out as my cells burn off the bindings of my curse. Maybe the freedom won't last, but if it lasts long enough for me to shift forms, I will have an advantage.

Minutes later, or perhaps it is forever, I sag against my shoulders and pant for breath as a man. The cool air inside the shack kisses the sweat on my flesh and my entire body shivers.

It takes a moment for the interior of the room to stop spinning before I can rise to take a knee.

Keyla is naked and unconscious next to me. Shockingly, our connection is so tightly linked I pulled her from her shift as well.

If I were the prince I once was, I would avert my gaze and play the part of a titled gentleman.

I'm not that male any longer.

I've not felt the comfort of a woman's flesh since my capture. And even if I had… Keyla is exceptional.

Perfectly smooth, tanned skin. Slender legs muscled with the strength of her animal side. Softly round hips. A perfect ass. Her breasts are larger than I expected, for her athletic frame—no complaint there. And around her neck, she wears the most amazing tattoo.

It must hold symbolic meaning because her brother, the Wolf King wears one as well.

She is breathtaking.

Heat scorches my body, my exposed skin tingling as if I've stepped too close to an open flame. The burning isn't wholly unpleasant, I'm thankful we're alone and she's unconscious because there's no hiding the effect she has on me.

Unlike the arousal I get at the prospect of fighting and fucking Rhylan, there is nothing dark and violent in this erection. This cockstand is all about attraction and the promise of the unadulterated pleasure fated mates share.

In a life that has taken too much, could the universe finally be giving me something back?

"Little Wolf? Are you alright?"

She's shivering in the aftermath of my forced shift and I search for a way to warm her. Spotting a stack of bedding near the door, I grab a thick blanket and drape it over her.

Stepping back, I pace the room and flex mental muscles that were locked down for the past two years. The fae population here is largely wildlings. I can't access their thoughts, but I can sense them.

Most minds are in REM sleep, the mixed frequency brainwave activity bringing on a variety of dream states. My eyes flutter in my sockets at the thought of dream walking again. It's been *so* long.

I look at Keyla lying there and wonder...

I shouldn't...

If she's to be my mate, I should respect her privacy enough not to invade her unconscious mind... shouldn't I? But we're not going to be mates in the romantic sense, so what's the harm in taking a quick spin around her innermost thoughts?

I return to where she's lying so peacefully and sit on the floor next to her. One might think it's prudent to access her dreams to know her.

After all, I'm supposed to trust her.

Doubtful. I gave up on trusting people years ago.

I study the inked mark on my palm.

Soul seared. If we're truly mirrored souls would I be angry if the roles were reversed, and she entered my dreams? No, I wouldn't.

Would I understand if she needed to build her mental acuity and test her limits after being drained and blocked for years? Yes, I would.

I flex my fingers against the burn. It will continue to burn until we complete our mating—the universe's way to force our hand. I'm not sure it will work this time around. Keyla seems no more interested in mating me than I am in mating her.

I tried the true love road once.

Once is enough.

Still, it's strange to hold a female in my gaze and know she belongs there. I try not to read too much into the sensation, knowing it's the power of the searing.

I lift her hand and press our palms together. The burning subsides instantly.

Burying the fingers of my free hand into the dark lengths of her hair, I brush it away from her face. My mate turns into a wolf.

How sexy is that?

Her wolf is magnificent—as white as the purest snow on the cliff tops. She is magnificent as a woman as well... if I were interested in that kind of a relationship... which I'm not... and she's not.

Her eyes flutter open, and I give her a moment to orient herself. "Welcome back. I'm sorry. Forcing my shift affected you as well. I didn't realize it would."

She sits up and flashes on the khaki pants and cream sweater she had on this afternoon when we met at the food table. Funny.

I didn't notice how aggressively that sweater clings to her lush curves then.

Again. No complaint.

"What happened? Kotah said the searing would keep us in wildling form for days if not longer."

"Normally, it would have, but I figured it would be easier for me to assert our wishes as a man, so I accessed the magic of my heritage. I didn't realize you would be dragged along. I'm sorry. That had to be excruciating."

She rakes her fingers through her long, chestnut hair and seems to push away the fog of her mind. "It's over now and I'm thankful to be able to voice my thoughts. Wow. You're really naked."

I look down at myself and nod. "I am."

Her cheeks flush pink and I chuckle. "Unfortunately manifesting the clothes I wore when I transformed isn't a skill of mine. I'm not a wildling. I'm a blood-cursed mind guardian. I'm surprised you're embarrassed. I thought wildlings are immune to nakedness."

She hands me the blanket I covered her with and averts her gaze. "Unaffected—usually. Immune—not today. When the naked guy six inches away from me is the male the universe wants me to mate, getting up close and personal with his lovely male parts is overwhelming."

I chuckle and wrap my hips with the blanket. "Well, you're safe. My lovely male parts are now covered. Fight the urge to pin me down and take advantage of me."

She grins. "I'll do my best."

A knock at the door shatters the moment and brings my attention to the world outside.

We're not ready, but there's nothing to be done.

"Keyla, there's so much to tell you and no time. Whoever's at the door, ask them in. I need clothes and we need to follow the demand of our searing."

I drop the blanket and pad quickly to stand behind the door. "Destiny calls, Little Wolf. Let's go find out what it wants."

Doc

I plod back through the trees of the Pennsylvania forest, intent on speaking to my girl. Enough is enough. Brant was right—I need answers. I may not have been ready to get them a few hours ago when he wanted me to, but I'm ready now.

Yes, it's the middle of the night... but maybe Calli was right and Keyla running from me is like when she first resurrected as the phoenix.

That morning, Brant left me high and dry in the middle of the back pasture. He said he felt the pull of his call. He totally zoned out and had nothing on his mind except closing the distance to his mate.

That could explain her reaction. It would also go a long way in patching up my pride.

Only one way to find out.

I follow the scent of my girl to the cabin closest to the portal gate. Makes sense. The two of them were wildly annoyed to be kept here against their will, so they probably tucked them away in the closest spot.

One of Hawk's men is on the door. Makes sense. The wolf wouldn't leave his sister unattended and Hawk covers the needs of all his mates.

"Hey." I recognize the guy from this afternoon, from when we were unloading the supplies. "How's things?"

"Quiet now."

"Quiet inside too?"

"Haven't heard a peep."

I'm surprised... like really surprised. I figured they'd try to bust out or be pacing or snarling. "Are you sure everything's alright?"

He nods. "Yeah, like I said, quiet."

Uh-huh, we seem to have covered that quite thoroughly. "And you've been here the whole time?"

He tilts his head back and forth. "One of the dragons came by and needed to check in on his prince. Stayed right here though."

"And did the dragon go inside?"

He looks at me and makes a weird face. "No. He just looked inside... No. He didn't go in... I'm pretty sure."

I track the fog of confusion on the guy's face over whether the dragon did or didn't head inside and it brings the hair up on the back of my neck.

"He did," he says definitively. "See, he's over there at the queen's cabin. That giant tree man made the purple queen from StoneHaven and the Past Prima each a cabin more fittingly royal before he left for the other realm."

I step off the platform and ease back until I see the dragon shifter standing guard. When I lift my chin, he casts me an arrogant glare. I'm not sure if it's a dragon thing or a Stone-Haven guard thing or what, but those boys are cocky assholes.

I return my attention to Keyla's cabin. My Spidey-senses are tingling all over and I have a sinking feeling. "Are you sure it was the same dragon that looked in? You know there are two of them, yeah?"

"Yeah, it was that guy. I recognize him."

"And you know they're identical twins?"

The guy's face falls. "I did *not* know that."

I scratch the side of my head and sigh. "Would you mind opening up? I don't have to go in or disturb them, but I'm having a hard time believing they went in there and curled up for a quiet evening."

He looks toward Hawk and Kotah's cabin. "Maybe you should come back in the morning."

My bear doesn't appreciate the brush-off, but I get it. No soldier wants to disregard orders or worse, have to wake up your boss because something went off the rails during his watch.

"They told you to keep me out, yeah?"

"And they were clear."

"Dude, I get it. I lost my shit but I'm calm now. I've got a seriously bad feeling about this and think you should at least look inside. My girl's in there and if there's a situation that needs to be addressed, we need to figure that out."

"Mr. Barron said not to bother them."

I nod. "I'll take the heat if there's blowback from Hawk. Maybe you're right… maybe they're just sawing logs and sacked out after an emotional day but if they're not… Hawk and the Fae Prime will want to know."

He seems to consider my words and then flicks his hand to shoo me away from the door. Fine. I'm not trying to bust in on them. He can check. I hop off the platform and step back to give him space.

He grips the doorknob and waits.

There's no growling, so maybe they are asleep. As quietly as possible, he opens the door and peers into the darkness.

I shift to get a view inside.

Someone's lying under a blanket but it's not Keyla or the demon dog boy. My worst fear springs to life as I realize what's happened. "It's the dragon. He never made it out of there."

Rushing forward, I kneel on the ground and pull the blanket back to make sure he's not injured.

"And he's really fucking naked."

"You're sure?"

"That he's naked?"

The guard huffs. "No, that he never left here. I distinctly remember him leaving."

I grip the guy's shoulder and give him a shake. "Dragon. Wake up." It takes a bit of work, but eventually, he starts to rouse.

He starts to sit up and then winces and cradles his head in his hands. "Slecking hell, what happened?"

I back up and give the guy some space. "You tell us. Keyla and her cursed object are supposed to be in here. Instead, we've got a naked surfer dude."

"They're gone?" He searches the stark interior as if there was anywhere for them to hide. The scene is literally four walls and plywood for a floor and ceiling. "Slecking hell."

Agreed. "Where are they, dude? The guard says you came and went and nothing else happened."

The kid curses. "Assuming the pounding in my cranium isn't due to the change in air pressure from our realm to here or a sign I'm having an aneurysm, I'd say Prince Creed regained access to his powers."

He presses his fingers together and then pushes them into his mouth. He blows like he's letting off a whistle, and I expect the sound to break the silence.

Nope. All remains quiet.

A moment later, Viking bookmark number two jogs into the cabin. "What's the issue? Why are you naked? You look like you're going to hurl up your intestines."

"I'm having a moment."

Hawk's guard looks from the new arrival to our man down and exhales. "The two people I'm supposed to be guarding are gone and now I have to tell our king his sister is missing."

Dragon Two looks around and now he might also hurl up his intestines. "Creed's gone?"

The weird vibe flowing between them makes me wonder

what I'm missing but honestly, I don't give a fuck. My only thought is about where Keyla is and that she's safe.

If that opal-eyed motherfucker has done something to her, I will rip him to shreds. I don't care that his beast is scaled like a giant lizard, rip him to shreds.

"How long ago do you think they left?" I ask. "When did you come to check in on them?"

Dragon One gets up, looks down at his junk, and curses. "The slecking bastard took my clothes."

"Yeah, thus the comments about your nakedness. Focus. How long ago did they leave?"

He fingers through his long, blond hair and flips the stuff off his eyes. Hey, he does have eyes. "Hard to say. You only have one moon. I left Vik guarding the queen, walked the perimeter, and then checked in here."

Vikarus curses. "That was hours ago. He brain-wiped you right out."

The naked one, Rhylan, lets off a curse of frustration and then scowls at his brother. "It's worse than that. He infiltrated my mind first. He knows everything."

"Knows what?" I ask.

Vik curses and starts to pace. "What do we do?"

Rhylan looks at the guard. "Get me some clothes and tell the military man who shut down the gate we need him."

"Lukas? Why?"

"Because with what Creed now knows, there's no way he's still in this realm. He's gone back to Dornte and he's hours ahead of us."

"They can't be gone. The gate was shut down."

The guy gives me a derisive scowl. "Creed is a mind guardian and has an eidetic memory. He knows how to work portal technology. There's no way they're still here. Get me the man in charge."

Bullshit. They can't be gone. This guy's trying to con me into opening the gate and letting them leave.

Bolting outside, I sift through the air, trying to pick up Keyla's scent from a couple of hours ago. Finding her scent isn't the problem. Sifting through the overlapping trails to find the one I need is.

Getting Kotah up to help would be the easiest and quickest way to address the situation, but I don't have it in me to deal with other people right now.

Instead, I impress the importance of the situation on my bear and let him do his thing. It's frustrating at first, but after a long moment of trial and error, I find it.

Stomping off the platform of the cabin, I track Keyla's scent back to the portal gate. It's strongest here.

I think back to the chaos of when they locked eyes and dropped. We came from the opposite direction and went straight to the food table. There's no way she touched the control panel of the portal gate.

Damn it. The dragon's right.

With no other choice but to start waking people up, I head to Brant's cabin. If Keyla made it through the portal gate with that demon freak, there's no time to lose waiting until morning.

I have to find my princess.

CHAPTER SEVEN

Keyla

The moment Creed and I cross the threshold of the rift and begin our journey from my realm to Creed's, my skin crawls with the needling of a million nettles. I hiss and rub my arms. "Ow, that's terrible."

Creed grimaces beside me and nods. "It will get worse before it gets better, I'm afraid."

Wonderful.

I scan the tunnel we're in and frown. If my skin's going to crawl like this, we need to keep moving.

I wasn't sold on Creed's plan to run off on our own when we launched this race between worlds but honestly, after seeing him in action I'm thinking it might go better than I expected. He handled the dragon, the guard, then accessed the power of the Portal Gate, then got us through the rift without issue.

That's the kind of efficiency we need.

The sooner we find the source of our destiny calling the sooner I'll know what it all means and what can be done about me and Doc.

About five yards in, the tunnel explodes into a tube of kaleidoscope colors and I feel like we've entered some kind of alternate universe.

Which, I suppose, we have.

I lift my hand to shield my eyes from the brilliant colors stretching out before us. It seems like there's no end. I don't like it.

My wolf snarls and I fight her need to shift. I growl, tensing to run forward and find the exit.

Creed squeezes my hand. "Shhh... Little Wolf. Deep breaths. We'll be through this soon enough. Do you see the golden glow in the distance?"

I focus my heightened gaze on the center of the tunnel ahead. "Yes."

"That's the other side. That's the gate opening that leads us to Dornte."

I squeeze his hand, the connection of skin-to-skin a glorious relief from the pain pulsing in my palm. When I first shifted back from my wolf, it was there, a blue faery medallion branded into my palm.

Creed says it's the universe's way to prod us to consummate our bonding. The pain it causes will continue to increase in intensity until we physically acknowledge our union and accept our place together.

Neither of us is keen on being forced to have sex, but until we figure out a way around that, it's palm-to-palm so we can both function.

It feels disloyal to Doc to even accept this much closeness with him, but at the same time, it's the most natural sensation. Something electric happens when I'm near Creed. Something so powerful it makes my heart hammer. Holding his hand seems innocuous against the potential of that. Besides, it's the only relief from the burning of the universe's mating game power play.

I'll make Doc understand.

Pushing that out of my mind, I lock my sights on the growing golden glow at the other end of the bridge between realms and quicken my stride.

Creed is a foot taller than me and has long legs. I have to jog to keep up with him, which is fine because we're in a hurry.

"How did you know how to access the gate system and bring the bridge back online?"

He casts me a sidelong glance. "My father believed no ruler can lead his people successfully if he doesn't understand the trials of the citizens. Growing up, I spent time working in the palace kitchen, the armory, the stables, and almost every other area of the realm, including our portal transport hub."

"I'm impressed. Our fathers saw things very differently. Mine saw everyone around him as beneath him—Kotah and I included. He and Mother moved to the palace and left us on our family lands to be raised by packmates. They believed it to be undignified having children underfoot while ruling a realm."

He frowns. "Having royal parents is a kind of dysfunctional few people understand."

"Very true. I figure if we are the realm's perfect mirror of one another I now have at least one person other than Kotah who might understand."

"I suppose that's true. Me, and my sister, Honor."

I know that up until twelve hours ago, I never knew he existed, but there's a part of me that recognizes a kindred spirit in him. Maybe the universe was right, and we'll be a great team to pull the realms together.

"Tell me about StoneHaven," I say, our steps falling into a synchronized rhythm. "Everything I know about your realm was learned from old stories or legends from books written before the wars. What happened after access to our realm was closed off?"

We jog for a little longer while he seems to consider what to say. "By the end of the Wars of Power, what was once known as StoneHaven was divided into four primary quadrants, Dornte, Clarinta, Travon, and Rames."

"So, you don't call it StoneHaven anymore?"

"The original StoneHaven capital city still exists but now it stands as a historical site and is the location of the great archive libraries and the historical treasures. It's located in a pocket of land at the meeting point of all four quadrants."

StoneHaven isn't StoneHaven. Good to know.

"How do the quadrants work?"

"Each of the four quadrants has a major city sector as well as outskirt towns, communities, and rural food processing. Beyond the agricultural lands there are fringe zones, and then out further still, the badlands. The way the geography works, the badlands of each quadrant connect to the badlands of the other sectors."

I cast a sideways glance, trying my best not to notice how poised and regal Creed is. His voice does sinful things to my insides but when I look at him, I'm able to keep reality in check.

He's not Doc. I love Doc.

Any physical draw I feel for Prince Creed is simply the result of the searing. It's not real.

It's not real that when I hear his voice my core begins to weep.

It's not real that now that the searing is settling into my blood and bones, I can't look at Creed without my body tingling to life.

None of it is real.

The problem is that it feels very real.

Does he feel it too? Does it matter?

We made it clear at the beginning that our pairing won't have anything to do with an emotional relationship. We're partners. We're an arranged marriage paired together by the universe to strengthen the two realms.

He has Bloom—his love.

I think about Kotah and how beautifully he, Calli, Hawk, Brant, and Jaxx have built a love that extends beyond the normal social boundaries.

Can I pair with Creed to unite the realms and mate Doc to fill my heart? Is it wrong to wonder? Is it naïve to think I might convince Creed to make it work?

Creed brushes his thumb absently over my hand and I swallow. The friction of flesh on flesh sends a pang of pleasure straight to my nipples.

Which is utterly inappropriate given the situation. I reclaim my hand and end the contact before I become a beacon of hormones. As a ruse, I smooth my hair and scratch the side of my cheek.

Creed doesn't seem to notice… which is good.

Lifting my chin, I focus on that golden glow at the end of the tunnel. "What are fringe zones and badlands like? Are they really bad?"

"Fringe zones aren't too bad. That's where we run penal colonies and prisons. It's also where people can choose to live lawless if they don't want to abide by the regulations of quadrant civilization."

"It sounds like what humans call the Wild West," I say, imagining life without rules. Part of me loves the idea. The smarter part of me knows the rules and laws of society keep people safe. "I don't suppose we'll go to the fringe lands or the badlands, will we?"

Creed shakes his head, his silver hair fluttering against his shoulders. "Likely not, but since I don't know what the beacon going off inside us is, I don't know where it's located. I can't say for certain. In normal life and circumstances, no, you'd never find yourself there."

That satisfies me for the time being. "And the badlands? What are they like?"

"The badlands are areas that suffered the most devastation during the wars. They are the battlegrounds left in ruin."

"Are they inhabited?"

Creed nods. "They're occupied by dangerous overlords, lawless rebels, mercenaries, and those so badly mutated and tainted by the magic unleashed in the wars they can no longer function in society."

I frown. "And how close are these badlands to where you reside in Dornte?"

Creed waves away the concern. "Not close at all. Most civilians of the sector cities live and die having never been to the fringe lands let alone the badlands. Even as the prince of the Dornte quadrant, I've only ever met a handful of people from the badlands and only because they were sent as envoys to the castle."

That doesn't make me feel much better. "My concerns stem both from a safety standpoint as well as a royal worried for the safety of a land's citizens."

Creed nods. "I respect that, believe me. The first chance we get, I will appoint you a personal guard. When I'm not with you, I want to ensure you are safe and well taken care of."

A new guard? The idea is offensive to me.

I blink against the sting of tears and fight to hold my composure. Chin up, eyes forward, I lock down the ache in my chest.

"What's wrong? I felt the sharp shift in your mental pathways. I said something that hurt you. What is it?"

I swallow and shake my head. "It's nothing. You were telling me about the badlands?"

He catches my hand and pulls me to a stop. "It's not nothing. Something I said upset you. Please tell me what it was. For this to work, we have to build trust. To do that, we have to be honest and aware of each other's thoughts and needs."

I meet his gaze. His eyes are so strange—two stones of ebony coal when he's a man and two swirling, glittering opals when he's his animal form. Something about his gaze doesn't feel right. "To be honest with you means I will hurt you and I don't wish to do that."

"Hurt me how?"

I stare at the golden light ahead and blink back the moisture in my eyes. "You mentioned me needing a bodyguard. My love, Dillan... my bear... he's a military soldier who became a doctor when he returned from service. Over the past three months, while we accompanied Kotah, Calli, and the others on their quest to create the rift between our worlds, Dillan was my bodyguard. It's how we got to know one another and fall in love."

His opaque gaze betrays nothing except for his intelligence and a quiet brooding. "And you expect this to hurt me why?"

"Because I want *him* as my bodyguard. I want him to be here with us and help me on our quest like Calli's mates helped her on theirs. Couldn't we find a way to make it work with you and me together to unite the realms but for me to keep Doc and you to keep Bloom?"

His lips curl in a smirk that holds no amusement. "You want both of us? Do I seem like the kind of man who shares?"

I step back, suddenly remembering I don't know this man or anything about him or how he treats people. "I thought... if your heart is with another..."

"Bloom's dead. Laryssa's men slaughtered her two years ago. All I've had since then are violent images and the guilt of knowing she died trying to help me."

I press a hand against my throat as the acrid burn of agony hemorrhages off him. "I'm sorry. I didn't know."

"Now you do. For two years I've been bound and tortured to endure—until tonight with you. Now I have a chance. In a world that has done nothing but take from me, am I supposed to give up the one thing the universe gave me in return? I don't fucking think so."

The burning from our mating mark is growing to painful levels once again. I clench my hand into a fist to keep from whimpering. "I shouldn't have said anything. You asked and I thought... It was stupid. I apologize."

He stares at me for a long moment and then curses. "Don't apologize. You're right. I asked, you resisted, and I prodded for you to tell me. You warned me I wouldn't like what you had to say, and you were right. I don't. Now, let's get out of this tunnel."

Creed

Keyla and I arrive at the end of the rift tunnel in silence and step into the gold-gilded portal room. The trylle on duty isn't the same male who opened our way into the realm yesterday, so perhaps we can get out of here without too many probing questions.

"Welcome back, my prince," he says leaning to the side to improve his view of the tunnel behind us. "Are Her Majesty and the dragons with you?"

"They'll be along in a few hours." I lock gazes with him and reach into his mind. "I brought the young lady back early because I wish to take her to the castle and get her settled in her new home. It makes perfect sense."

"It makes perfect sense," he repeats.

"And since the two of us are unescorted, we should, of course, take a security tablet and a sidearm to ensure our safety."

"Of course," he says, grabbing his keycard and striding over to the storage lockers against the wall. After passing his card over the sensor and keying in his code, he hands me the weapon and a datapad.

"You've been a great help, sir. When the queen returns, she and the dragons will likely kill you—I *am* sorry about that. I hope it's not the case, but if that's the way of things, you will die with honor and secure in the knowledge your family's future is ensured. You are at peace with that because you are a patriot."

He nods. "I am a patriot."

I catch a glimpse of the horror in Keyla's eyes but don't have time to stop and justify myself. The burn of the mating brand is already becoming painful again.

She's as stubborn as she is tough and isn't complaining. I know I pissed her off when I snapped about her including her bear in our relationship, so I suppose it's up to me to offer her the olive branch.

To that end, I hold out my hand. "We need to keep moving. Come, our adventure is in its infancy and there is much to do."

She gestures to leave but doesn't accept the offering of my hand. It seems she'd rather suffer than touch me.

She might be smarter than I gave her credit for.

The portal room we arrived in is one of many, so our next challenge is to navigate our way out of the building without being detained by Laryssa's enforcers.

Keyla jogs along, tucked close behind my right hip. Her positioning is telling. It speaks of her being trained to be guarded by a right-handed warrior. I happen to be ambidextrous, but it's good to know she's not a totally pampered princess.

I take the first corridor and push through the door to the stairwell. Once we're secured inside, I hold out my hand again and this time she sets her brand to land on mine. The relief from the burning is exquisite.

When the ache dissolves completely, I reclaim my hand and flip the datapad over. The back panel only opens until the inhibitor strap restricts access. I give it a yank and force off the panel door to open things up.

"Are you truly leaving that man to be killed by the queen for aiding us?"

"Unfortunately, his fate was set the moment we came through the rift. Maybe the dragons will lie and he won't die, I don't know. Either way, he'll be at peace."

"But you manipulated his mind."

"Your point?"

"You could've sent him somewhere safe to hide. You could've erased his memory of us so he couldn't be held responsible for our escape. You chose to leave him there to die with a smile on his face."

I stop what I'm doing and meet her censure. "Laryssa had all personnel chipped when she took over. There is nowhere he could go where she wouldn't find him. The logs will show he was there when we came through. A quick inventory will make it apparent that he armed us with tools to evade her. The best I could do was offer him a peaceful death if it should come to that."

When nothing more is said on the matter, I figure she's either furious or has accepted my explanation. Resuming my task, I frown at how tiny the tracking chip is within the workings of the datapad. "You don't have any fine tools on you, do you?"

Keyla leans in to look. Pulling a pin from her hair clip, she hands it to me. "Will this help?"

"It might." I try not to notice how her hair falls loose now that it's no longer contained. Try… and fail. Bloom had lovely hair too, although she possessed explosively spikey ebony hair. It was sassy and unruly like her.

I try to remember her like that and not how I last saw her, lifeless on the stone courtyard. I never even got to say goodbye. Laryssa's forces dragged me away and straight to the blood witch to be bound and brutalized.

Without my powers and with the lives of my mother and

sister hanging in the balance, I could never truly rebel. Until now.

Resurrecting my tinkering skills from when I was an ill-behaved boy, I use Keyla's hairpin to pry the tracking chip loose and fling it toward the stairs.

With that taken care of, I hand Keyla the tablet and the access door to put back together. Next, I pull out the weapon. "Now we take the tracker out of our blaster."

"She certainly enjoys tracking things."

I nod and make quick work of removing our weapon from her network. "I should probably warn you, I'm chipped as well. That will be our first stop."

"I thought we'd follow the call of our searing."

I reclaim the datapad and turn it on. "It won't do us any good to search the city for the source of our call if I show up on every enforcer's nav screen, now will it? First my chip. Then our quest."

I punch in Rhylan's officer code and call up the security alerts for the city. "Good. All seems quiet so far. Let's go."

Keyla looks annoyed. At least this time when I extend my hand to her, she relents and meets my palm with her own.

"I understand that your world has been at peace for the past centuries, but this world has not. You must trust me, Little Wolf. I will keep us safe and we *will* unite the realms, but to do that, we need to stay alive and stay out of Laryssa's control."

She considers that for a moment and then straightens. "Fine. How do we get that chip out of you?"

CHAPTER EIGHT

Doc

I knock on the door to the cabin Brant and his mates are in, my body vibrating while my bear paces within. Brant opens the door, naked and unabashed. When he sees it's me, he runs his fingers through his long, brown hair and yawns. "Someone better be dead."

"How about missing? Creed and Keyla accessed the gate and are gone."

"What?" Kotah extricates himself from the fated mate pile-up on the bedding platform and sifts through a pile of clothes to find his pants. "How could they? Lukas shut the gate down."

"Dragon boy here—"

"Rhylan," he snaps.

I wave that away. "Fine. Rhylan here says the black-eyed prince has lots of hidden talents. One of them being an extensive understanding of portal gate procedures."

"Fuck me," Hawk hisses as he, Calli, and Jaxx all get out of bed. "Where's Lukas?"

"He's downloading the gate's activity log with the other

dragon. And fun fact, their first reaction to realizing the two were gone was pissing themselves that when the queen finds out the silver-haired freak ditched them, their lives will be forfeit."

"Why?" Calli pulls her long, blonde hair free from the collar of her shirt and comes out from behind Brant who's playing the part of her dressing screen. "Creed's her son. If he took off, it's on him not them."

Kotah frowns and waves us inside. "Brant, light the lamp." He takes a step closer and breathes deep into his lungs. "Rhylan, explain to me what's happened."

The blond steps inside and looks like he'd rather be anywhere but here. "The two of them are gone. The bear and your man out there are wasting my time. I need to get through the gate and find them before the queen realizes they've escaped."

"Escaped?" Hawk says, pulling on his shirt.

"I mean left. The prince shouldn't be on his own. Dornte isn't as safe as it once was. Which is why Vikarus and I were named his guards."

Calli chuffs. "Even without the wildling sense of heightened smell, I call bullshit. You can't con a con, blondie. There's more to this and we all know it. I vote we keep the gate locked until you spill it."

The dragon takes two swift steps toward Calli and he's swept off his feet by both Brant and Jaxx. He lets off a pained grunt as he's slammed back and pinned to the wall with the force of two mated males.

"Don't you fucking advance on our female," Brant says, his eyes flipping gold. "Apologize to the lady."

Rhylan closes his eyes and lets off a stream of curses. "My desperation got the better of me for a moment. My apologies. You must understand, Queen Laryssa is not a benevolent ruler. Those who fail her die no matter what the reason."

"And you're not Creed's bodyguards," Hawk says, "You're his prison guards."

The muscles in Rhylan's jaw flex, but honestly, time is ticking. He feels it. I feel it. If he needs to find Creed before the queen finds out, he'll be highly motivated.

That works for me.

"You are correct. Creed is the rightful heir to the Dornte throne. Queen Laryssa usurped the quadrant. He is her prisoner, and she enjoys taking him out and flashing him around as her prize. It is our job to ensure he stays in line."

"So, what happened?" Kotah asks.

"The soul searing seems to have negated the queen's lockout of his powers."

"Which are?" Jaxx asks.

"Creed, as all of the Thornebane line, is a powerful mind guardian. He has the ability to manipulate synapses, alter memories, enter dreams, implant suggestions into the minds of others... and a host of other things."

"Implant suggestions?" My bear lets off a roar. "Is that why she ran off with him? He brainwashed her?"

The dragon shakes his head. "That's doubtful. Prince Creed is an honorable male. If this was solely about him gaining his freedom, he would've left on his own. The fact that he took his mate with him—"

"—that beast is *not* her mate," I shout.

Kotah turns on me. "That *male* is the fated mate of my sister. We don't know much about him, granted, but you won't speak ill of him when he's not here to defend himself. The searing is a predestined bonding by the fae universe, as was my own. Keyla and Creed expressed their need to return to the other side of the rift the moment they were bound. Perhaps we should leave them to discover their destiny."

"I'm surprised at you, Nakotah," his mother says, striding into the mix. The woman, still wearing her coronation gown from three days ago, refuses to change into anything as common as the clothes Calli offered her.

I step to the side to let her pass. Fuck me. At this rate, we'll never catch up to them.

"You have never been overly invested when it comes to politics, Nakotah, but I thought you at least cared about your sister."

Kotah's expression tightens but he seems otherwise unaffected. "I do care about her, Mother. More than you ever understood. I also respect the woman she has become. Keyla has been chosen for something beyond our understanding, the same as I. No doubt she will rise to unimagined heights and make us all proud."

Calli takes his hand and smiles. "Well said, Wolf."

He dips his chin. "Keyla supported us in our journey, and we will support her in hers. She won't face this alone. We'll leave now and ensure her safety."

The former prima sweeps a hand over her scalp, smoothing her long, chestnut hair. After living with the comforts of the Fae Palace for decades, a few days in the forest has nearly done her in. "Foolishness. Your duty as Prime began the moment your father passed. Your place is here."

Kotah stands before his mother, naked except for the unbuttoned jeans barely clinging to his slim hips. He tosses his hair behind his shoulder and it falls loose to his waist. "The rift is open. It is understandable I would travel to the other realm and assess what happened there over the past centuries. Queen Laryssa spins fanciful tales of her realm and her rule, but I would be remiss to not investigate for myself."

"Then send a team."

"I'm not sending a team to watch over my sister in a foreign land." He steps back and gestures to the Prima's aid. "Raven call for the royal jet. Hawk's helicopter pilot will fly the two of you to the local airstrip in the morning. You are returning to the palace—"

"—And you are not?"

"Not yet." He reaches to the floor to pick up his shirt. When he straightens, he pulls it over his head in slow, deliberate movements. "Return to the palace, Mother. Rest and assess the state of things. I'll return as quickly as possible."

"You would leave this realm without leadership?"

He lifts his chin and offers her a patient smile. "The Fae Council is on hiatus and the royal visitations are paused. There's nothing to be done for the next few days and you are capable of overseeing the palace until my return. In the meantime, I will help Doc see to Keyla's well-being. Once we assess her situation, we can decide what to do next."

I rub the warmth in my chest. Having the Fae Prime pushing the search for his sister will be a helluva lot more effective than me searching a world I know nothing about all alone.

Thank you, Kotah.

He dips his chin as if he knows what I'm thinking. "Now, back to bed, Mother. In the morning, I'll need you to handle Laryssa. Use your considerable powers of delegation and persuasion to convince her that, on a whim, I demanded Creed take me to see the city where my sister is destined to live. Stress my irrational impatience and that I simply wouldn't be delayed."

"And that one of the guards escorted us," Calli adds.

"Not us, kitten," Jaxx says. "You and I will stay here and oversee the gate from this side. We don't know what they'll be walking into over there. I'm not comfortable having you and the cub there for first contact."

Calli's eyes dance with the fire within her. "Don't coddle me, Puss."

Hawk shakes his head. "No, Jaxx is right. With the gate opening up, I can't leave yet either. Lukas has a team tracking down my idiot half-brother. I need to find out more about what my father was up to and how it works into the Fae Realm. He made inroads with Laryssa and planned things beyond the gate opening. We need to figure out what."

Calli shakes her head. "Doc can't go himself."

"You're right, Spitfire. Kotah and Brant should escort Doc and we'll get things sorted here and follow. It's a sound decision both tactically and for the safety of all involved."

Kotah nods. "Agreed. One of the dragon twins will escort Brant, Doc, and I while the others remain here to work out establishing and securing the portal gate."

Keyla's mother looks at her son and frowns. "I don't like this. To have not one but both of my children off acting wild in the name of destiny's call is embarrassing. What am I supposed to say to people when they comment?"

Kotah shrugs. "We are the Prime family. People don't get to comment on us or what destiny might have in store for us."

The Prima's look of indignation is priceless. Kotah truly is coming into his own. It's a beautiful thing to see.

"Now, it's time for us to finish getting dressed so we can set off. Keyla and Creed have a head start. We've got realms to explore and destinies to discover."

Keyla

The building housing the portal gate is the local transportation hub for the Dornte quadrant. Once we descend to the ground level, we stand in the stairwell and look out into the open atrium of the main floor. That's when I get the first sense of how big it is... and round.

It feels like the Roman Colosseum where the walls arch around in a giant circle and through each of the archways people are being transported to other places within the realm.

The entire place is built out of caramel and beige stone that sparkles as moonlight pierces four large skylights above. Its open and opulent detailing holds endless character which is reflected in huge chandeliers and carved statues set in sunken nooks.

"Wow, this place is beautiful."

His gaze narrows on me like I'm missing the point. "We need to mask our appearance, not admire the architecture. The silver hair of the Thornbane family isn't something people miss. I need a cloak."

Well fine. There ends my sightseeing opportunity. "I realize you're stressed, but you don't need to be brusque. Do you have a lost and found here?"

His gaze narrows. "What do you mean?"

"A bin where workers deposit lost or forgotten clothing to be claimed at a later date."

He straightens. "I don't know. Is that something a place like this would have in your world?"

"It is." I search the bustle of the main floor and it reminds me of an airport terminal. I suppose, in a way, that's exactly what it is.

I catch sight of a person in uniform entering what looks to be a washroom and I release his hand. "You stay here, and I'll go find out what I can."

"Go? You can't go out there."

I laugh. "No, *you* can't go out there. I can. Trust me, tall, light, and miserable. I've got this."

I strike off, Creed's hissed protestations following me for a moment before they're swallowed by the buzz of the crowd. I try not to draw attention to myself, and thankfully, with this being a central travel hub, people seem accustomed to all kinds of different travelers.

As I make my way, I marvel at all the different races of fae here. Some of them, I learned about during my studies as a child. Others are completely new to me. The fae races allowed to migrate into the Human Realm were humanoid or able to glamor themselves to fit in.

These people are not.

They range from one foot tall to ten, wings fluttering, horns curling, magic sparking...

My gaze catches on a woman who's half white and half blue. The division of color runs straight down the center of her forehead, down her nose, and I assume all the way down her body.

Her husband's coloring is the same but opposite. I wonder if that is an indication of gender or simply a coincidence. Either way... it's fascinating.

Ducking into the open archway where the worker disappeared, I'm gratified to find out I was right. It *is* a washroom. I take advantage of the facilities while I can, wash up quickly, and look around to find the attendant.

"Excuse me."

I smile at the person who turns unsure if it's a man or a woman. The waif-like citizen has pale blue skin with green, seaweed hair and is so androgynous, there's no chance for me to guess gender... assuming there is a gender to guess. Maybe not.

Xe is still staring, so I get back to my point.

"When I came through here the other day, I set down my traveling cloak and walked off without it. Where would I find the lost items bin?"

The worker frowns but straightens and sets down the cleaning supplies. "A cloak you say. Come along."

I follow, trying not to stare, but xe is so uniquely beautiful, it's difficult. We leave the washroom and cross the polished floor toward the other side of the gatehouse.

My hand is starting to burn but I try not to think about it. The sooner we get Creed covered up, the sooner we'll be on our way.

"Have a look here." I'm directed to a cabinet on the wall

between two archways. "If it's not here, it's likely been claimed by someone who needs it more than you."

I open the cabinet doors and smile. "Fair enough. Thank you. I'll have a look. Don't let me keep you from your duties."

When xe leaves, I assess the trove of items. After a bit of snooping and a fair bit of rummaging, I'm rewarded tenfold.

Jackpot.

I grab a leather satchel, stuff in a few things that might work to our advantage, and then select two cloaks. The half-length plum one, I swing over my shoulders and fasten with the silver buckle, the black, full-length one, I roll up and stuff into the satchel.

"Voila," I say, pulling out the weighty black cloak when I'm back in the stairwell with Creed.

He makes quick work of putting it on and then raises the hood to ensure his long, silver hair is tucked away. "Well done."

"I also found this and thought it might be helpful."

"What's that for?"

"It's a belt."

He chuckles. "I see that it's a belt but why do you think I need it? Rhylan and I wear the same size."

"For your blaster. I thought it would be less conspicuous in the street than you walking around with a silver space blaster in your hand."

"A silver space blaster?"

I chuckle. "Are you making fun of me?"

"Maybe a little." He takes the belt, and although he wraps the belt around his hips, I know he's only doing it for my sake. "Alright. Can we go now?"

When he reaches out, I catch his palm with mine and roll my eyes. "The fact that you find any of this funny suggests you've been a prisoner too long."

His smile dims a little, as he nods. "That's absolutely true but until you broke through the bitch queen's lockout protocols, I didn't have any other options."

I shrug. "Well, at least something good came out of the destruction of my life."

He squeezes my hand and tugs me out of the stairwell. "And it's only the first day. Who knows what else fate has in store for us tomorrow."

Fate. Yeah, who knows?

The two of us exit the portal station hand-in-hand and are lost among the crowd of citizens. We shuffle down the front steps and I get my first look at Dornte.

"It's amazing."

I can't read what's upsetting him now. He's scowling at the traffic and the high-rises and the foot traffic moving all around us. "If we survive what comes next, I'll give you the royal tour. For now, let's stay ahead of my jailors, shall we?"

"Do you think they've discovered us missing yet?" My belly twists when I think about Doc finding out we ran away together. He'll be so hurt and think I've betrayed him.

"We should have until morning. Your brother told everyone to back off and leave us alone and I left Rhy sleeping like a baby. Unless something unexpected happened, we'll be hours ahead of the dragons."

Good. That's good. "So, where to first?"

He points toward what looks like a train platform by the curb of the street. The cars here are more like hover crafts and by the surge of energy I feel as we get closer, they're powered by magic.

That beats fossil fuels by a long shot.

Say goodbye to global warming.

As we draw near the street, a monorail train slows down and stops with nothing more than a whirling hum. When the doors open, Creed pulls me in behind him and points at a group of empty seats at the back of the car.

The people already on the train pay little attention to us. Just a couple of cloak-wearing transit passengers.

Nothing to see here.

We sit down and the pounding of my heart surprises me. I didn't realize I was so wound up. I close my eyes and draw a deep breath to steady myself.

Everything about this feels so awkward and wrong.

I'm in a foreign realm with a mating bond burning in my palm, a beacon summoning me toward who knows what, a future unfolding I don't want, and I'm holding the hand of the wrong man.

Yet the universe says he is the right man.

The train jostles into motion and the hum gets us moving again. The city of Dornte streaks by in colorful swipes of lights —vehicles, billboards, and signs. The buildings zip past in a shiny golden blur.

"I've never spent any considerable time in a city. In our realm, fae populations are secret and pocketed so most of us live in rural towns and out-of-the-way forests. This is blowing my mind. So many fae."

He arches a silver brow, a subtle look of disappointment marring his face. "Unfortunately, we'll be navigating back alleys and shadows until I can get the tracker out of me. It won't be the best representation of my kingdom."

The train stops and lets on a group of mid-twenties night-goers. They're wearing worn, grungy rags and have colorful smears marking their cheekbones, brows, and bald heads. At first glance, I'd say they were homeless, but I think that's the look they're trying for.

When they turn our way and eye us up, Creed straightens in his seat and shifts his hand under the fabric of his cloak.

"Don't get any ideas, mates," Creed says, his voice carrying an almost hypnotic command. "There's nothing we have that you want."

"Slecking mind slut. You can hide under a hood but your brain hacks don't work on us."

Creed slides his hand free of the cloak and sets the silver blaster on his thigh. It's aimed toward them and they stop their advance. "This will work on you though, won't it? Shall we test it out and see?"

The male in the lead considers that for a beat and then decides we're not that interesting after all.

"We're getting off on the next stop," Creed says, as the group turns. "You and your friends won't be joining us. Are we clear?"

The leader dips his chin. "Crystal, you black-eyed freak."

CHAPTER NINE

Doc

The next fifteen minutes pass in a flurry of purpose. I grab Keyla's backpack and stuff some of my clothes in with her things and sling it over my shoulder. If that motherfucker brainwashed her into running off with him, he'll regret it.

The good part about living out of a duffle bag is that it doesn't take long to get gone when the shit hits.

Striding out of the cabin, I cross the encampment and meet everyone at the control console. The power of the rift has been released and the air is shimmering with the potential of the magical bridge between two realms.

"Are we ready to blow this place?" I ask.

Hawk nods. "We'll give you as much time as we can in the morning. Lukas and I will be busy with surprise maintenance first thing and who knows when we'll get the console back online."

"Thanks, man."

He winks. "No worries. If Keyla's mate is targeted for death simply for being the rightful heir, and the universe put us on team Thornebane, I figure we're meant to step in to set things right."

"Agreed," Calli says, munching on a granola bar. "That's my take on things too."

I'm not sure how Rhylan feels about Kotah and his Guardian mates taking a stand in the politics of his realm. There's obviously something he finds unsettling about the idea, but he's keeping his own counsel on that.

Outwardly, though, he's toned down the arrogance.

I'm not sure if that's a good sign or not.

"Alright, mates," Brant says. "Hold down the fort. If you don't hear from us in a few days, come find us."

Jaxx chuckles. "Just search the strange new world and come to your rescue?"

Brant nods. "That's what we do, isn't it?"

As much as they're joking, that is what the guardian mates do.

"Alright," Calli says, gesturing toward the undulation of energy. "Safe travels and successful hunting. We love you, boys."

Creed

When the transport shuttle glides to a stop, I escort Keyla into the street and glance up at the sky. "The second moon will be out within the hour, we have to hurry."

"What does the second moon coming out mean?"

"Right. Sorry. Laryssa imposes a curfew during the latter half of the evening. Once the second moon is out, citizens have fifteen minutes to get off the streets."

Keyla hustles along beside me, her short stride forcing her to jog. I'm of mixed opinion on that. I don't like pushing her to run, but the bounce and sway of her breasts are distracting in the best possible way.

I wasn't lying to her when I spoke of my heart belonging to Bloom. It does... it did... it should. She died for me and we had something special. Maybe she'll always have domain over my heart, but right now, it's not my heart that's speaking loudest.

I wish I could be the man Keyla deserves.

When the queen's enforcers killed Bloom, they killed something in me as well. Since then, the only sexual pleasures I've had are by my hand with memories of better times swirling in my mind and the tainted moments of enemies with benefits with Rhylan.

Fucking dragon.

No. It's not his fault I feel betrayed—it's my own.

Tasked to keep me in line, every time I escaped, they dragged me back and ratted me out.

They *are* the enemy.

That's never been so clear to me as it is tonight. When I scanned his memories for information about my mother and sister, every ounce of trust I'd foolishly placed in our shared moments was destroyed.

"Are you alright?"

I'm jarred out of my musings and follow the concerned words to the kind eyes of my mate. "Of course. Why do you ask?"

"Because I was suddenly washed with anger and betrayal. Our emotions seem to be linked—at least the strong ones."

I chuff. "You're imagining things that aren't there."

She frowns. "You don't have to tell me, but I know what I felt. I learned a lot by watching my brother navigate his mating. They are linked like we are. They feel what the others feel, they know the heart and soul of each other, and they had to learn to respect that connection, so no one got hurt or felt vulnerable."

I tug her down a dark side street toward the illegal gaming hall I hope is still in business. "I don't feel vulnerable."

"If you say so. Just know when things get away on you, I'm here and I'll listen without judgment."

I groan and roll my eyes. "If this pairing is to do either of us any good, you need to talk less. You are the reason I feel angry and betrayed. Less of you means I'll be less angry."

The flash of hurt in her eyes pierces my cold, dark heart. I curse myself. I have no idea why the universe decided to link the two of us together, but it was a mistake.

My days of being the sweet prince are over.

Tenderness has slowly been beaten out of me over the past two years. My heart was left bleeding out on the courtyard stone.

I point to the 'Do not Disturb' sign on the door.

"Enough chatter. I need you to stay quiet and let me handle things. You're out of your depths here, Princess. You're just along for the ride."

"Fuck you, Creed Thornbane. You need to pull your ego out of your ass and realize there are two people in this mating clusterfuck."

I blink. "I didn't realize you have such a mouth on you, mate."

"I've lived the past three months with my brother and his warrior mates. I picked up a few things."

Keyla

As Creed knocks on the door in the back alley, I rein in my tirade and applaud myself. Taking a page out of Calli's book not only made me sound badass, but it felt really good. I lift my chin and strengthen my resolve.

Apparently, even mirrored souls aren't a perfect match. Fine. If he doesn't want to open up and be honest with me, I can do the same. He needs me to stay quiet. Quiet is what I'll be.

Cue the sound of silence.

When no one answers his knock, Creed turns his fist sideways and bounces it off the door without stopping. The pounding drones on in the night until I'm sure it'll be the police coming and no one inside.

"What is your—" The man who opens the door stops speaking the moment Creed pulls back the hood of his cloak. "Majesty. You're alive... and here... how?"

Creed replaces his hood and grins. "If you invite us inside, I'll tell you, Riven. But first, there's the matter of a pesky tracker in my ass. I'm assuming you can help me out with that?"

"Of course, sir. Come. My apologies."

The three of us move inside and pass through a warehouse modified to act as a private casino. There are gaming tables and rowdy patrons and plenty of drinks and girls being passed around. My first thought is how much Brant and Jaxx would like a place like this.

My next thought is how Creed knows about it.

What kind of prince is he?

If he frequents places like this, his life as a royal was vastly different from the life Kotah and I lived.

And how does he know this man—Riven?

I study the man and find his appearance and manner unsettling. Even if he didn't have little devil horns and pointed ears, I doubt I'd find him any more comforting.

We're led past the gambling activities and through a corridor to a set of stairs. When we reach the top of the stairs, Riven pushes the door open and ushers us inside a loft bachelor's apartment that smells of cats and sweaty gym bags. "First things first. Drop your pants."

I blink, my mind stumbling on that as Creed tosses his cloak over the back of the sofa and toes off his boots.

I can't imagine anyone saying something like that to Kotah when he was a prince. Now, however, I wouldn't be surprised to hear one of his mates speak to him like that, but that's altogether different.

Creed seems to take no offense.

He hands me his blaster and I set it on the top of my duffle. Then, he drops his leather pants to the floor and stretches out on his belly on the man's dining room table.

"I'm relieved to find you a creature of habit, Riven. If you weren't here, my escape from the clutches of the bitch queen would be much more difficult."

I turn on my heel and give the man my back, images of him naked already burned into my memory from the cabin. Creed naked doesn't matter because I love Doc.

It means nothing.

The tingling of my skin means nothing.

The tightening of my nipples means nothing.

The warmth gathering in my core means nothing.

"So that's where you've been?" Riven says, returning from the bedroom with a dark red medical bag in hand. "The queen has had you all this time?"

"I'm surprised you aren't aware. She takes me out and parades me like her prized puppet every couple of months. Why don't you know that? You normally have your thumbs in everyone's assholes."

Riven waves that away and unzips the bag. "When the shit hit and the quadrant was lost, I took an extended vacation. My sister married a fire master from Rames. I spent a few months with her and then moved around the other quadrants. I've only been back a week or so."

"Then it's good fortune for me, you're here to aid your prince when needed."

There's a strange echo of emotion in Creed's words and I turn back to see if I can tell what's happening.

Riven is a slight man, certainly no physical match for Creed, yet the prince is holding himself with an air of caution. Maybe Riven's species holds hidden strengths.

If Kotah were here, he'd likely know what species of fae he is, but I don't. If I'm to spend time here, I'll have to catch up on things like that to be of any value.

Despite Creed's insult—I'm *not* along for the ride.

The two of them continue to speak in pleasantries and I get over my prudish ideals. Creed is stretched out on the table, propped up on his elbows, his bare backside up for Riven to access.

From where the man is working, the tracker isn't so much in his ass, as Creed said, but below the small of his back—awfully close to the base of his spine.

It strikes me then, Creed's right.

I have no idea what he's been through or what we're facing. I saw the images of his capture. The violence and the bloodshed he endured. Hell, he has a tracker embedded at the base of his spine to keep him as her prisoner.

I suppose him feeling angry and betrayed is perfectly normal. Laryssa took away his choices and then our searing did that again. No wonder he resents me being here and chiming in with my opinions.

I'm the princess who lives the charmed life.

That's what it must look like from the outside.

In truth, it's been a week since my father died. Less than four days since my brother's coronation was attacked and my mother kidnapped. And less than twenty-four hours since my life was taken from me.

I move to the seating area and lower myself into the time-beaten recliner. I haven't eaten or slept in far too long and the sight of Riven slicing into Creed's back is making me slightly nauseous.

If that's a charmed life, someone else can have it.

I miss my bear.

Raising my burning palm to stare at the branding mark my tears sting hotter. Having my love for Doc forfeited to save lives and unite two realms is something I can understand. Sacrifice for the many. It's not that different from Kotah accepting his place as Fae Prime.

I hate it and would change it if I had the choice, but I don't. So, I accept my duty. But being forced to give up the man I love for another who doesn't want me around seems cruel.

"Hey, Little Wolf," Creed says, squatting down in front of me. "Why the tears?"

I swipe the corner of my cloak across my eyes and draw a deep breath. "Don't concern yourself. We don't need to talk. I'm just along for the ride, remember?"

My words hit him harder than I expect. "And I'm—What did your bear brother-in-law call me?—a royal asshat. I'm not sure what it means but it sounds pretty accurate."

I swallow and straighten. "Are you unchipped? Our destiny awaits. Don't want to miss out on that."

I don't mean for my words to come out with such a venomous bite, but they do. He frowns but doesn't say anything. Why would he?

He's as trapped and angry as I am.

There's a long pause when I think he might say something but then he grabs the security tablet and starts tapping the screen. When he's finished, he sighs and sets it back into the bag. "Destiny is next. There's one thing I need to do first."

Creed grips his blaster, and in a move so fast my mind blurs to catch up, he turns and fires.

Riven is struck by the blast square in the chest. He drops to the floor, a look of stunned surprise etched in his eyes.

I squeal and cover my mouth. "Why did you do that? Isn't he your friend?"

Creed arches a silver brow. "It's adorable you think people in our position in life can have friends. No. Riven was my father's political advisor and he colluded with Laryssa to aid in the crown being overthrown."

"Did you read that in his mind?"

"No. I can't read him. It just makes sense. He survived the infiltration of the castle which means one of two things: he either fled like a coward and left us to be captured and murdered *or* he was part of Laryssa's team of traitors and granted a pardon."

"He said he fled to another quadrant."

"A definite lie. I've played bone sigils against him enough times to recognize his bluff. He was dirty."

I look at the man lying dead on the floor. "But he helped you. Did he deserve to die?"

"He did because he didn't." Creed rushes over to the table and holds up the bloody scalpel. "He said he removed the chip but I'm still showing up on the security tablet. Which means he lied. You're up."

"Me? You want me to cut the tracking chip away from your spine?"

He nods and drops his leathers once again. "If you want to live freely beyond the next ten minutes, it's our only option."

Ten minutes. "I wish Doc were here."

Creed frowns. "Throwing your not-quite-a-lover in my face isn't helpful in this moment, Princess."

I storm over and take the scalpel out of his hand. "My not-quite-a-lover is an emergency medic and a doctor. He was forever patching up my brother and his mates during their quest. Stop belittling me. You said we were going to be partners and respect one another."

Creed climbs onto the table and offers me a sad smile over

his shoulder. "I'm sorry. I have two years of torture and anger inside me and am out of practice being civil. You're right, having your doctor friend here would be an advantage at this moment, but he's not, so it falls to you. Please remove the bandage and get that tracker chip out of me so we can be on our way."

I'm still shaking and angry, so when I grab the edge of the bandage taped to his skin, I rip it hard and fast.

Creed hisses, his butt cheeks clenching into two beautifully toned globes. "Alright, yes. I deserved that. Try not to take your hostilities out on me for the next part though, if you don't mind."

I frown and look at the stitched incision at the base of his spine. "I'm not as tall as Riven. Can you scootch closer to me, please?"

Creed shuffles to the edge of the table, and when I lean forward to look directly down on the incision, I'm in direct contact with a whole lot of Creed's very fine ass. The contact unleashes a wave of sexual impulses and my wolf growls. The sound is long and gruff and I'm not sure whether it's a good or bad thing.

I'm so confused.

"Focus. Try not to think about anything but what we're doing right now. Do you see the chip? It'll be the only thing inside the incision that looks like it doesn't belong there."

I look at the tray of tools Riven used and pick up another to help me prop open the cut. "I see it."

"Take the forceps and see if you can pull it free. It shouldn't be attached to anything. They just shoot it in with an injector gun, so it should be sitting there unencumbered."

Thank goodness. I grab the little silver tongs and do my best to grab hold of the little metal square. "My hands are shaking so badly. I'm afraid I'm going to sever your spine or something horrible."

"You're not going to paralyze me." He chuckles and his body quakes with amusement.

"Stop that! I could hurt you. Stay still."

"You won't hurt me. Just pluck it out and we'll be done. On three. Have you got it?"

I pinch the little prongs and swallow. "I think so."

"Okay. One... Two... Three."

I wince and pull the little wafer of technology free from the living tissue that has grown to claim it like weeds in a garden.

"Did you close your eyes while operating on me?"

I open them then and meet the amusement in his gaze. "Maybe. I don't remember. My head's spinning."

He shakes his head and chuckles. "Paste the bandage back on so we can go."

I drop the chip and the tools back onto the tray and replace his bandage. "What about the stitches. Riven stitched you back up."

"Do you know how to suture a wound?"

"No."

He smiles. "Then we'll go with the bandage. Time is ticking anyway."

I get him put back together and he rolls off the table. He straightens right in front of me and I studiously look up at his eyes. "I'll get the bag and your blaster."

I skirt around him and focus on not forgetting anything. When I turn back, he's got his pants back on and is buckling his boots. Before he grabs his cloak, he grabs the weapon's belt off the hook by the door and straps it around his hips. "I'm trading up. No offense meant to the little belt you found me."

"None taken." What looks like a man's wallet is lying on the end table by the sofa. I hold it up for Creed to inspect. "Is any of this of use?"

He selects a couple of shiny cards and leaves the rest. With that taken care of, he wraps his cloak around his shoulders and secures the brooch. "We'll go up to the roof and across to the next building before going down the back way. It's safer to assume Riven tipped off security when he went into his bedroom."

I hold out my hand and let him lead the way. the moment our palms meet, I sigh feeling much better about things than when we arrived.

CHAPTER TEN

Rhy

So that's it. I'm dead. I'll get put down for failing the queen and the last chance to restore the Silverwing name will fail. Shadowcaster knew assigning us to Laryssa's psychotic rule would either end in our termination or our disgrace and he was right. It's the only reason he named us for royal guardianship.

Born to one of the oldest families in the most powerful wildling race, Vik and I should be kings. We would be if our Dragon Alpha, Shadowcaster, hadn't tried to claim our mother... or if our father hadn't challenged him in a battle to keep her... and lost.

Duty and love aside, him being too proud to share his female left our mother widowed and claimed by the Dragon Alpha anyway, and Vik and I as the piece of shit boys sired by the traitor who died.

That's a tough reputation to live with.

Now, unless I can pull a miracle out of my ass and recover

Creed before Laryssa figures out what happened tonight, it's over.

The Silverwing Dragon Clan is ruined.

I appreciate the Wolf King covering up the escape by saying I escorted all of them back to the castle, but if she discovers the truth, she'll kill me for failing and our family name will remain tarnished for eternity.

My dragon is raging to fly. If the portal tunnel between worlds was big enough for my dragon, I'd shift and fly to the other end.

It's not. So, I'm stuck suffering the walk of shame. I didn't realize he'd gotten his powers back. I let him get too close. Will letting my guard down with Creed cost Vik his life, too?

That's even worse.

I can handle falling on the sword for my failure, but Vik shouldn't have to pay the ultimate price as well.

The soles of my boots thunk with each stormy step because as stupid as it is, dying and sentencing my twin to death isn't what's eating at me the most.

The look in Creed's eyes when he scanned my memories for information about his mother and his sister hollowed me out. Yeah, I lied to him for two years. His mother never survived the initial uprising and his sister escaped for almost a year and was only recaptured a few weeks ago.

Leveraging his family was Laryssa's best chance of keeping him in line.

In a better realm, he would've been allowed to mourn the loss of his mother. It might've brought him comfort to know both his parents died the same day. He could've taken strength in the knowledge they roam the Sacred Grove together enjoying the afterlife.

Instead, he was told she lived as Laryssa's captive—his sister too.

Only, Honor truly did survive and is being held as insurance.

Yes, his younger sister escaped for a few months, but she was tracked down and recaptured. She's now back under Laryssa's thumb.

"Where do you think Creed will take Keyla?" the Wolf King asks.

I push down my self-disgust and answer honestly. "I don't know. If this were two days ago, I'd say he'd seek out where the queen is holding his mother and sister but there's something more happening. He told his wolf that they would seek out the beacon calling them."

"Beacon?" Doc snaps. "What does that mean? What beacon? What's calling them?"

"I can't say. As you can imagine, I'm the last person he would confide in."

I regret the lie the moment it's out of my lips.

StoneHaven doesn't have many wildlings—Vik and I have long been a rarity in that way. It's afforded me the luxury of lying when needed, which I admit is often.

Animal wildlings were able to blend in with human society so, at the time when the Wars of Power began, most of them moved out of the realm. Dragons weren't included in that emigration, so we learned to think of ourselves as unique.

Now I have to remember that all of these men smell lies as keenly as Vik and I do.

"How are you planning on tracking them down?" the big bear asks.

"The prince was fitted with a tracking chip. Once we arrive in the portal hub, I'll reclaim my security tablet and track him down."

"Does he know he's LoJacked?"

"He does. It's how we found him on the occasions he's managed to escape."

"How quickly did you find him?"

"Almost immediately. Vikarus and I are very good at our jobs."

"Hashtag usually," the big bear says.

I throw the massive warrior a look. "We had no way to know the aftereffects of the searing would break the queen's tether."

Kotah frowns. "It sounds like you're defending your right to hold the rightful prince hostage and torture him. If that is the case, we're not your target audience."

I huff and focus on the golden doorway ahead. Slecking Guardians. So righteous. They have no idea the lengths people will go to in order to survive.

The king is studying me and doesn't look impressed by what he sees. "In any case, with at least a four-hour lead, I'd consider the tracking chip option removed from the board. Prince Creed strikes me as a man who thinks on his feet."

"He's a mind guardian. What do you expect?"

When nothing comes back to me, I figure they are clueless about what that even means. Oh, well. They'll figure it out sooner or later.

"Tell us about StoneHaven and what to expect," big bear says.

I ramble off the basic structure of our realm, the four quadrants, the ancient city of StoneHaven, and assure them that other than clothing, the abundance of nature, and some minor differences like food and currency the realms aren't much different.

"I'm surprised things are so similar," little bear says.

"The realms didn't evolve as independently of one another as you might think."

"What do you mean?" Wolf King asks.

"Once the wars ended, a traveler program was started at StoneHaven. We've been sending consciousness into your realm for over a century. It's kind of the rage here to use the curse words and turns of phrase the travelers report. The Human Realm is quite a fad."

"Consciousness?" Kotah asks.

Seriously? These people are more human than fae. Don't they know anything about our abilities?

"Certain races of fae carry a psychogenesis gene that allows them to project their conscious mind into another living being. For years the archivists at StoneHaven sent envoys into your realm to learn about how fae were evolving."

The bears look to their king and something passes between them. They don't let me in on their little secret and honestly, I don't care.

"Do your travelers influence things in our realm?" big bear asks.

"They're not supposed to, no. It's an observation program. Why?"

The brute shrugs and shakes his head. "No reason, just getting the lay of the land. What about travel within the realm. How does that work?"

"Each quadrant is self-contained with badland on the outer rim that connects with the badland of its neighboring quadrant. In the city centers, there is a portal hub to allow travel to the other quadrants."

"And other portal stations to travel within quadrants as well?"

"That's right."

Kotah nods. "We have a permanent portal station in the Prime Palace which I expect serves much the same purpose."

"Likely the same idea."

The big bear is grimacing and rubbing his massively muscled arms. "Will portal gate travel always take this long and be this uncomfortable?"

"No. Once your gatehouse is fully operational and the links and bridges are fully established, it'll be the same as the local and cross-country portal experiences."

The king nods. "That's one of the things we'll establish while we're here. We'll work on locking in the coordinates for the gates on this side of the realm."

"Gates, plural?" Brant asks. "I thought we eliminated all the destroyed gates as viable options."

"On our side, yes. Hawk's father set us back on that front. For now, we must be content with setting up each of the four quadrant city centers to portal travelers to the Pennsylvania property."

The black bear shrugs. "It's better than what we've had for the past couple of hundred years."

"True that. Beggars can't be choosers."

"Besides," Kotah says, "it's not a bad thing to have limitations in the beginning."

Brant nods. "It makes it easier to shut things down if uniting the realms goes to shit and blows up in our face."

I see the chance to play both sides of this to my advantage and take it. "A friendly warning. With Queen Laryssa in possession of the only linked bridge to your realm, it likely *will* blow up in your face. She's a bully but she's not stupid. She understands power and how to keep it for herself. It's how she took the throne in the first place."

Kotah gives me an appraising gaze. "We'll take that under advisement. Thank you, Rhylan."

I nod. "If you like, and please don't tell the queen I offered to help you, I will set you up with a liaison to contact the other quadrants when we arrive. If I were you, I'd take advantage of the few hours head start you have as well."

"My priority is my sister," Kotah says.

To my surprise, it's the brunette brute who takes the bait. "If it's time-sensitive, I'll make the first inquiries while you three search for Keyla."

"That won't work." I offer them what I hope is a convincing look of apology. "The four crowns don't deal with intermediaries. It's one of the reasons Dornte fell. The leaders of the other cities will only deal directly with those of their level of authority."

The wolf king doesn't seem to like that, but hey, the needs of the many before the needs of the few, right?

In the end, he nods. "Alright, I'll take care of contacting the leaders of the other quadrants. I need to be kept informed of everything that's happening, though, and I will join you once you have a lead on where they are."

Good. If I can get some of them focused on other things, I'll have fewer in my way when I have to take down Creed. "Fair enough. I'll make it happen."

Creed

We exit the alleyway behind Riven's apartment and merge with the traffic of the street at the same time the second moon comes out from behind the clouds. The first klaxon sounds and my mind scrambles. "We need to find somewhere to stay for the night."

"Please let it be somewhere with food."

I look at Keyla and curse. "I'm sorry. This all started when you came to the food table. You never did get anything to eat."

"You either. Aren't you hungry too?"

"Now that I'm thinking about it, I am. Funny. While my life was exploding around me, I lost track of that."

I guide her to the street, and we hop onto the last shuttle. The doors close behind us and the hum of the engine pulls us away from the curb.

"We'll get as far away from here as we can in the time we have left. Then we'll tuck away for the night."

Keyla settles onto the bench beside me and releases my

hand. She's still got blood on her fingers and I realize she's looking ragged—beautiful, but ragged.

"We can't go anywhere they'd think to look based on knowing me. You should pick the place and I'll make it happen."

Keyla's gaze flares wide. "I should pick? I've never been to this realm before."

"Exactly my point. When we get off the train, you lead the way."

We sit in silence for the next few blocks and the shuttle doesn't stop. At this time of night, it doesn't stop to let people on unless someone is standing on the platform or buzzes to get off.

When the second klaxon sounds, I stand and watch my city go by. It's been years since I was able to be alone on the streets and I've missed it. After a few more blocks, I hit the button to stop. When the doors open, I step off and reach back to take Keyla's hand.

It's gratifying how easily she comes to me.

I lead her off the platform and over to the nearest line of buildings. "Alright, what do you think? Where do you think we should go?"

"Do you have hostels or drop-in centers for people without homes or money?"

"They're run by the queen and her men. We'd have to scan in. You won't scan and I can't."

She looks around for a moment and points to where three people have flipped up a service cover and are climbing down into the underground. "What's that?"

"That's an access point to the city underground."

"Who are those people?"

"I don't know. Citizens who don't have a place to live above ground?"

"Are they violent citizens?"

"No. Just poor, displaced, or those who choose not to live on the grid of the city."

She nods. "Then that's where we'll go. After all, we're poor and displaced at the moment."

I shake my head. "But you're the Prime Princess of your realm. Why would you want to go down there, let alone plan to sleep down there?"

"Because people who don't have much are often the most understanding of hard times. The citizens down there won't be Laryssa collaborators. Those people will have homes and privileges. The citizens in the underground are more likely people who don't fit into the current social system."

The final klaxon sounds and I shrug. "We're out of time. Into the underground it is. Pull your hood up."

I pull my hood further forward as well and escort her across the sidewalk and over to the service cover. Using the pull rope, I haul back the metal lid and take a look down the ladder. "I'll go first."

She shakes her head. "Don't be silly. You need to close that cover. If I pull it forward it will fall and crack me in the head."

I don't like the idea of her going down first. "We don't know what's down there."

"If you're worried about me, don't be. I'm not as fragile as I look. I've had martial arts training and weapons masters my entire life. Despite you thinking my life has been all strawberries and orgasms, it hasn't been."

The countdown beeps start sounding off and I curse. "We're officially out of time. Hurry."

Keyla swings her legs around and starts lowering herself down the ladder. I follow close behind. After I lower the service cover, I make quick work of dropping to the ground to join her.

"Hands up." There's a green-skinned, wrinkle-faced trylle, pointing his weapon at us. "Who are you? Why are you here?"

I'm inching my hand toward my hip when Keyla throws me a disapproving look and steps between us.

"Hello. My name is Nakeyla and this is Creed. We've had a very trying day and need a place to lay our heads for the night. If you could extend us the kindness, we would be forever grateful."

I shake my head. Does she truly believe that will—

"My name is Coal, of the underground clan of faery outcasts and unwanteds."

"It's lovely to meet you, Coal," Keyla says, offering the man a graceful little curtsy.

"You'd do well to stop pointing that weapon at my mate," I snap, the words ripping from my throat.

He must hear the violent truth of my warning because he gives me a dirty look and then lowers his aim. He doesn't sheath the weapon, but at least he won't accidentally fire and kill Keyla.

"Creed," a pixie woman with ombre blue hair says, fluttering silver wings. "You're named after our prince?"

Keyla smiles. "Actually, no. He *is* your prince and I just liberated him from his imprisonment from the queen usurper. Does that make us friend or foe?"

I blink at her. "Seriously?"

She grins. "Relax. I smelled the loyalty and admiration in the air when she mentioned your name. You're in no danger here."

The trylle man and the pixie woman turn disbelieving gazes on me and I pull back my hood. "Good evening. I apologize for invading your sanctuary, but as Keyla said, we've had a trying day and need a place to eat and sleep during the hours of curfew lockdown."

The two seem struck dumb, but that doesn't last long. Keyla giggles and drops the hood of her cloak back. "We haven't much to offer in exchange for hospitality at the moment, but I'm from the Human Realm and I'd be happy to tell you stories of what life is like there if you're interested to hear."

The trylle's head snaps back so suddenly he likely pulled something in his neck. "The Human Realm? How is that possible? Has the phoenix risen?"

Keyla nods. "She has. Her name is Calliope Tannis and she mated my brother, Nakotah. They opened the rift between worlds two days ago. And here we are."

I chuckle taking in the wonder and disbelief of our welcoming committee. The trylle holsters his weapon and gestures down the lamp-lit tunnel. "Come inside. The others will be so excited to hear the news."

CHAPTER ELEVEN

Creed

She's ridiculous. The ponytail princess barges into a community of people she knows nothing about and exposes our tender underbelly by telling them who we are and why we're vulnerable. Does the woman not have an ounce of self-preservation?

And yet, here we are—accepted into the fold.

We've been fed, given a pallet to sleep on in a private offshoot of the tunnel system, and she's enlightened them for an hour about life in her realm. They've kept her talking about what the phoenix is like, who the guardians turned out to be, and a million other things I never realized people cared about.

"And have you seen the phoenix in flight, Prince Creed?" a curvy gnome with orange eyes asks.

"I have, yes."

Keyla waits expectantly but I have no more to say on the matter. She flashes me a teasing smile and elaborates on my behalf. "Yes, Queen Laryssa commanded the dragons and Prince Creed to push their way through the rift and seize control."

"In true form," an old gnome says, stroking the silver strands of his beard.

"I hope you were able to shut her down," Coal says.

The group pauses as they realize the implication of that. To speak that kind of treason was a highly punishable offense. Laryssa doesn't allow dissension in her quadrant.

"No offense meant, Highness," the old guy chokes. "The hour is late, and I spoke out of turn. My apologies."

"No need to apologize," I assure him. "My support of the queen has been nothing but an act forced upon me by them leveraging my family's safety against my actions. And yes, to answer your question, the phoenix and her guardian mates made short work of us. In our defense though, it was five against three and we certainly weren't expecting a phoenix."

Keyla grins. "It's hard to prepare for Calli even if you are expecting her."

I smile. My mother was like that. Using the past tense in a sentence to describe my mother blindsides me and I drop my gaze to regroup.

"Creed? Are you alright?"

I meet her concern and force a smile. "Just tired."

Keyla's expression dims. I hate the sad disappointment in her eyes and hate it even more that I put it there.

"One day you'll realize I'm worth trusting. I look forward to having an honest conversation with you once you do."

I cast her an apologetic smile and release her hand to get settled on the pallet. Today is not that day. Unlike Nakeyla Northwood, my disposition isn't naturally moonbeams and chocolate. Too much has happened to have faith in people. Leaning back, I close my eyes.

We can't all be ponytail princesses.

I sigh, chastising myself. She has proven herself more than that today. I need to give her more credit.

"Alright," she says, beside me. "Enough for now, my friends.

We'll talk more when your prince has had a chance to rest. Thank you all again for your hospitality."

There's a scurry of bodies and then the pallet dips and she's lying against my side. She pulls a blanket over us and taps the back of my hand. "I think the only way we'll get any sleep is if we hold hands. Do you mind?"

"I do but it's not your fault and there's no one for me to fight about it, so here we are."

She stiffens. "Yes. Here we are."

I lace my fingers with hers and set our joined hands on my chest. "And to answer your question… when you mentioned Calli being a force, I thought about my mother. I didn't know she was dead until I read Rhylan's mind during our escape tonight. Laryssa has been using her capture to keep me in line. It makes sense she wouldn't allow them to tell me she was killed in the raid, but it caught me off guard."

She squeezes my hand, and her wide, brown eyes tear up. "My father died last week. He had been sick a long time, so it wasn't a surprise, but that doesn't make it hurt any less."

When she snuggles closer, I fight the urge to push her away. Instead, I brush my free hand down her shoulder. "I'm sorry. I didn't realize Kotah's ascension was so recent. He seems quite at home being your king."

"Not at all. He never wanted to be bound to a palace. His wolf is a wild spirit. He craves open spaces more than most. Political life is his worst nightmare. Still, my father passed and Kotah was his heir."

"Were you and your father close?"

She yawns and rests her cheek on my shoulder. "As close as he was capable of, I suppose."

The ache of unfulfilled need echoes in what's not said and my heart goes out to her. Perhaps not everything came easily for her after all.

Thinking about all the happy years our family spent together almost makes me feel guilty. "I'm sorry you're hurting. I must say, you hide it well."

"Years of practice. Mostly I think I'm handling it alright, and then there will be this flash of realization out of nowhere—I don't have a father anymore."

It's only been a couple of hours, but I've already had that moment.

"To the fae world he was the Fae Prime, but he was my father. He's gone and that's it. At times, I'm angry at myself and the people around me. Why doesn't the world feel more different without him? Shouldn't it? The man who sired me is gone."

Her anger stings me with a poignant familiarity. "The same thought has run through my mind since I found out. I have no parents. I'm an orphan. There's just me and Honor... and I don't even know where she is. I'm alone and my kingdom is in shambles."

"We'll find your sister and we'll figure out what to do about your kingdom." She shifts her cheek on my shirt and blinks up at me with more compassion than I can bear. "But don't think for a moment that you're alone. You're not."

Her conviction to stand at my side means more to me than I can fathom. "How do you do that?"

"Do what?"

"How can you speak about our pairing with such confidence? Twenty-four hours ago, you had your head and heart set on life with your bear. Me not being able to handle the mess that is my life is the reason you were torn from him. This searing is my fault."

Keyla's hand is warm on my cheek as she searches my expression. "You don't know that. Maybe the universe believes you need help and maybe not. That doesn't make this your fault."

"And yet, as upset as you are, you aren't fighting against me or what it means to be mine."

"That's because I see how important this is. When Kotah was bonded to Calli and the others they didn't see it at first. They knew the prophecy and what they needed to *do* but not what could *become*. They had no way to comprehend the depth and breadth their mating would affect them on a personal level."

I search the warmth of her gaze. There's something alluring dancing in her eyes. A promise? A challenge maybe. "What are you saying? Do you think we could be more than political allies? We agreed your heart was taken—"

"We did agree, and I *do* love Doc. I won't lie and deny there's more between us than a magic bond bringing us together. You're a good man, Creed Thornebane, handsome, proud, self-sacrificing, and strong. The universe declared us a true match. I admit, I'm attracted to you and wonder what else we could become."

She pushes up against me, the lush rounds of her breasts straining the front of her sweater. Her lips brush my cheek in a chaste show of affection, and I'm rendered dumbstruck.

In my lifetime of sexual encounters both meaningful and reckless, this moment stands out.

For the first time since the searing took us down, I wonder who I could be with her at my side. I need her to reclaim my kingdom, but maybe not only as my co-conspirator. Maybe she truly is meant to be my queen.

The thought scrambles my mind.

I hadn't thought that far, but now that I am... why didn't I consider it before?

The answer hits without warning—Bloom.

I pinch my eyes shut and ease back. Drawing a deep breath, I push down the piercing loss attached to losing her to the violence that lurks around a man in my position. I manage to collect myself but can still feel the sting of emotion threatening to surface.

It feels disloyal to be excited about Keyla being my queen when Bloom died trying to protect me.

How can I disregard what we shared for the potential of something new and shiny? What kind of a man does that make me?

My mind is whirling with thoughts of life and death and love and betrayal and there's too much to sort through. Having my powers back online has flooded my mind with the extra energy I was denied for two years.

It's a lot.

Keyla has stilled against me. When I meet her concerned gaze she offers me an apologetic smile. "Sorry. I guess I shouldn't have done that."

What is she—oh the kiss.

"No. It's been an emotional day. I'm sorry. The kiss was lovely and received with the warmest thanks. I'm simply over-whelmed."

When she shifts off my chest, I curse and fight the urge to pull her back. Thankfully, she isn't gone long. She resumes her place in the crook of my arm and pulls a blanket over our heads.

When the fabric settles over my face, I open my eyes. It's pitch dark. "What are you doing?"

"I'm inviting you into my privacy tent," she whispers. "Kotah and I used to hide under the blankets when we were discussing something unbecoming a royal. Instead of risking the censure of my mother or a governess, we whispered our private thoughts or cried or confessed our truths this way so no one could hold it against us later."

I bring her knuckles to my lips. "And what truths do you expect me to confess?"

"None. That's not how it works. You seemed to need a moment of privacy and I want to give it to you. Now you can be sad about your mom or angry about your kingdom or confused about our bonding without worrying people will see. You are Prince Creed, but you're also a man doing his best in a tough life."

I am. And if I'm being honest, my hurt, anger, and confusion are compounded with betrayal. Rhy knew about my mother and didn't tell me. Me being angry is stupid because he *couldn't* tell me....

What part of *enemies* with benefits did I miss?

I roll toward her in the darkness and press my lips to the side of her head. "Thank you, Little Wolf."

"I've got you, my prince."

"For better or worse, it seems."

"Let's try for better. I've had enough worse for this lifetime. I'm tired of it."

I nod under the fabric of the blanket and chuckle at the turn my life has taken. "Agreed. Let's try for better."

Doc

The four of us come through the portal gate and are met on the other end of the golden glow by the relief of our skin not stinging and my bear not trying to force a shift to bolt. The release in tension is a welcome bonus. With my anxiety worked up as it is, I'm fighting not to claw someone's throat out.

"How long ago did Prince Creed and his lady come through?" Rhylan asks the guy behind the console.

Their portal gate is fully built and, according to Rhylan, is one of many portal rooms in a building they call a portal hub.

"Sir?"

"Prince Creed came through here with a female. How long ago?"

The guy looks wholly confused. "Was it before my shift began?"

"Check the data logs. It's more likely he wiped your memory of his return."

The guy looks confused but when he checks the logs, he looks up and frowns. "I have the arrival of a Forest Lord and a young boy early in the evening."

Kotah nods. "That was Rowan and Yarko. The Forest Lord was anxious to return to this realm. He's been separated from his people for centuries."

The guard nods. "After that... huh, then I have two people four hours ago. That was during my shift, but I have no recollection."

Rhy rushes to a set of lockers and presses his thumb on the front screen of the door at the end of the row. The locker clicks open, and he pulls out a black weapons belt and what looks like a sci-fi silver blaster. Once he has those strapped across his hips, he removes a tablet and fires it up. "What time is it?"

"The second moon is out, sir. The first klaxon has rung."

"Good. I'll track his chip." Rhy taps the screen of his tablet and grins. "While that's uploading, I need you to call the portal hubs in Rames, Clarinta, and Travon. Tell whoever answers that the phoenix has risen and the prophesy has been realized. The Fae Prime of the Human Realm is here to establish the coordinates to the gateway bridges. They'll need to send ambassadors."

"Shall I do that now, sir, or wait until morning?"

Rhylan frowns and looks over to Kotah. "That's your call but once Queen Laryssa gets back here, things will get a lot more hostile and complicated."

Kotah frowns and meets Brant's gaze. They're obviously having a cranium-to-cranium convo and sorting out the best way to handle personal versus professional.

When they finish, Kotah nods and turns back to Rhylan and the console attendant. "I will work on making the necessary connections for the establishment of the Portal Gate. Brant and Doc will continue in the effort to track down my sister."

Rhylan nods. "I'll run you upstairs and get you set up in a management suite upstairs. I can have a liaison from the castle meet you here and he can walk you through who you're talking with and how best to approach the ambassadors from the other three quadrants."

"We can't wait," I say, my bear rearing up and roaring inside me again. "They already have a huge lead on us. I know the portal gate politics is important, but—"

Rhylan holds up his hands and shakes his shaggy blond hair. "No. We're not waiting. The nightly curfew is about to lock down the streets. Creed will either have to turn in for the night or risk tripping the citywide camera system."

I like the sound of that. "So, if civilians aren't allowed on the street at night, we have a chance to catch up with them and gain back some lost time."

"Yes. *We* have the advantage for the next six hours."

"Where do we start?"

He gestures for us to follow and heads out the doorway and down the corridor. "I've got a location on the prince's tracker. Odds are against it still being within him, but we might get lucky. If he wasn't able to find a doctor or the equipment needed before the klaxon sounded, he'll be stuck until morning."

"But we'll be able to move through the streets?"

"Yes. We'll activate the facial recognition program on the city cameras to search for him."

The dragon comes to the end of the corridor and into a round, stone atrium that during the day likely holds a thousand people easy. He banks right and starts climbing the open staircase two steps at a time toward the management suites.

Kotah nods. "Then let's not waste a moment."

Rhylan seems to agree. When he reaches the top landing, he presses his hand on a scanner beside a room plaque, and a metallic *click* unlatches the door. "Are you good to wait here on your own? You might have to entertain yourself for an hour or more. It'll take a bit to get envoys here from the other quadrants."

Kotah glances inside the private conference room and grins. "I'm sure I'll be fine."

Kotah hugs Brant and cups his chiseled jaw. "Be safe and good luck. Find her, Bear."

"Done deal. You take care of you, Wolf." When Brant steps back from his mate, he looks at me. "You ready for a night on the town?"

My bear lets off a long, throaty rumble. "Beyond ready. Let's find my girl."

CHAPTER TWELVE

Keyla

I startle awake with images of a massive midnight demon dog with opal eyes battling my beloved black bear. They growl and claw and tear at each other with a savagery I didn't think either possessed. And while my throaty screams fall on deaf ears, my father's pyre burns in the background.

I shiver, a cold chill locked in the center of my chest. Lying on my back on a thin but soft pallet, I pull my breath to the depth of my lungs.

It wasn't real.

In the darkness of an underground city tunnel, even with no lit lamps, I see as clearly as I would in full daylight. My vision is muted to gray, black, blue, and green, but it's enough to assure myself the scare was only a nightmare.

As my panic and heartache ebb away, I focus on what is real and what is not. I'm in the fae realm with Creed... I left Doc behind in the clearing of the Pennsylvanian forest and ran off with the man the universe says I'm destined to love.

I see the appeal. He has that wounded man of honor thing that sucks women in. As royals growing up in the dysfunction of royal life, we understand each other better than other members of our societies ever could.

But I love Doc.

I smile at the darkness, pleased that despite spending time with Creed and knowing what we could be, my feelings for Doc remain unshakeable.

I love Dillan Baskins...

But I feel things for Creed too.

As if he senses me thinking about him, he shifts beside me. His broad hips thrust tight against my thigh, a gentle snore vibrating warm against my neck.

I squeeze our joined hands and realize why I was shivering cold. My prince has stolen the blanket. I chuckle to myself, tug the fabric to cover me, and wriggle back a bit to take full advantage of his warmth.

His free arm, muscle-banded and heavy, is draped over my ribs, his hand cupping the round of my breast. It strikes me that I should be upset with the intimate contact. I'm not. If I'm honest, I understand what Doc was saying at the river about experiences expanding my understanding of what love is.

I was so sure I knew my body and mind, I didn't let the possibility of other options.

And then came Creed.

His morning wood is a full-sized redwood back there. He's grinding that erection against my leg and it isn't bothering me at all.

Unless I count being hot and bothered.

My dream makes sense now—the turmoil of two strong males tearing at one another. I'm sure my father's pyre was a remnant of our conversation before we gave in to sleep, so I discount that part and focus on the fight.

It doesn't have to be that way.

I've seen what Kotah's quint means to each of them. I want that. The thought of it is like caramel cake warm in my mouth.

It's gooey and so yummy.

Creed's hold on my breast is possessive. It sparks a heat in me I've only ever felt with Doc until now. I'm probably being influenced by the magic of the searing, but after seeing how happy Kotah is... do I care?

My brother will never regret allowing Calli, Hawk, Jaxx, and Brant into his bed. They have chemistry and passion. Each of them plays a different role in the relationship, but they work.

I think about our joined hands, amazed we managed to sleep as long as we did and not let go. Is that telling or just a reflex not to feel the pain of separation?

I squeeze his hand and his body tenses, tightening his embrace as if he doesn't want to let me go. Creed groans in his sleep and I freeze.

The pained sound resonates inside me and triggers my need to help him. He has suffered enough. That's why the universe stepped in. Whatever is meant to be, he can't manage it on his own. He needs me.

I breathe deep and pull his scent into my sinuses, filtering the gentle nuances of his flesh.

Creed carries the musky spice of a male who hasn't washed since fighting in a battle. His natural scent is infused with an unmistakable masculine power that is both from him and his species, as well as the faint trace of...

Oh? Really?

Having sex with one of his dragon guards isn't something I expected. I wouldn't have smelled it if I weren't lying with my face against him and studying every detail of his scent.

My heart thunders for a moment and I wonder if it was consensual. Is that one of the ways the queen has him tortured? My instinct says no.

I didn't pick up that level of emotion from him when he confronted the dragon during our escape.

Still... I'll watch the two of them together to get a clearer understanding of what he's been through.

Creed groans again and nuzzles his nose against the nape of my neck. His erection is becoming more demanding. I smile as my body responds in turn.

It's nice that he's hungry. I enjoy the desire.

I've told Doc he doesn't always need to treat me like a princess. He doesn't understand there are times when I want to simply be groped, pinned down, and consumed.

The thought of it hits me with a warmth low in my belly. I close my eyes and think about the hours Doc and I spent in the forest yesterday... his mouth on my core, licking through the heat he calls from me.

"Come for me, babe. Right into my mouth. Feed your male."

I swallow as a rush of sensation hits. The magic of the searing has me so keyed up.

The universe is trying to draw Creed and me into a physical bond. Maybe I can hold off better if I release some of the pent-up need.

Once the idea strikes, there's no second-guessing. My free hand slides under the blanket and I slip my hand down the front of my khakis. I undid the button to go to sleep, so it's easy to lower the zipper and slide my fingers beneath the silk of my panties.

Glancing beside me, I make sure Creed's asleep.

He is. His breathing is steady, the tense scowl he wears when awake nowhere in sight. Good to go.

The moment the tip of my finger slips between my folds and brushes my clit I shudder. I close my eyes and focus on staying quiet.

Gods, how is it possible that I'm so damp and ready?

Is it all the external influence of mating magic or does part of me want Creed. Want sex with him. Want sex with him *and* Dillan.

Yeah, I won't lie. I want that.

I see how Calli is with Brant, Jaxx, and Hawk and it's hot.

Closing my eyes, I imagine… Doc's worshipping attention to detail with Creed's aggressive, alpha assertion.

Circling the nub of engorged nerve endings, I coax the erotic keening. The sensation it releases is sharp and strong. I won't take long. My nipples are stiff and maybe Creed senses that in his sleep because he's palming me as his cock throbs harder.

My breath quickens and I widen my legs giving me better access. I quicken my ministrations, finding the perfect spot and increasing the pressure. The throbbing pulse of my pussy is delicious.

I need this.

I need to release some of this hunger so I can focus.

I need to honor my body's wants and not overthink.

Biting back the groan of my pending orgasm, I pinch my eyes closed and pant through my nose. Gods, it feels so good but my needs have never truly been met.

I imagine having a thick cock inside me. Pushing inside me, stretching my greedy, gripping muscles.

Damn it, why wouldn't Dillan just claim me?

The pain of that almost derails the building of my pleasure but I refuse to let my frustrations take hold.

Creed's grip on my breast tightens and I arch into his hold. Yes. My mind flips to images of Creed, naked and aggressive. He's a god of man, exotic and ripped. I even get hot when he's brusque with me. Not many people take on the princess. I like it.

I envision him taking me on in other ways.

Gripping my breast… pushing inside me.

I stiffen as my orgasm bears down on me. It's hot and

demanding and I picture Creed fucking me. He doesn't care that I'm a princess. He's rough and hungry and I'm his to claim.

I gasp and my release crests. It detonates in a hot flash and then the glorious pulse and throb take over.

Yes, this.

I lock my wolf's growl deep in my throat and focus on the sensation. Maybe it was wrong to get myself off in the arms of a stranger, but I don't care. Why should I feel guilty about taking care of myself?

I shouldn't. I don't.

I sag against the pallet and smile as my breathing settles and the sleepiness of the darkness returns.

I brush my leg against the cradle of Creed's hips and bite back a smile when a deep grumble of male appreciation perforates his sleep.

Considering his size and the level of testosterone it takes to fuel an alpha male of his standing, it's no surprise he's randy and ready to burst out of his leathers.

With slow, deliberate movement, I roll in his arms and lay face to face.

His expression is hard to read—harsh yet filled with longing. The tough warrior persona is gone, and I see the vulnerability he showed me last night.

Is it wrong to want to ease him a little?

His life changed two years ago when his parents were assassinated and Laryssa stole his crown.

He's faced that alone—until now. I'm here now and to the depth of my soul I know I am meant to be here, to help him, to be his partner... and mate.

It's not what I planned but there's no denying the sexual pull I feel to touch him and make that connection.

Creed

My consciousness rises in slow, hazy pulls toward alertness. Normally I don't sleep so deeply. I'm not sure what's happened at first. Was I drugged? I'm not in my bed? When a hand palms my aching cock, my eyes flip open but it's dark. Did Rhy fall asleep? We don't do the awkward morning after. Mostly because us fucking is a super-secret no-no that would likely get him killed.

So who's groping me?

It's dark, and my brain is still fogged.

"It's alright, my prince. It's me."

"Bloom?" The contact is lost, and the intake of breath has me confused. It takes a moment but my memory catches up with reality. "Shit. Sorry. I was still half asleep, Keyla."

I reach forward, seeking her out in the darkness as she retreats. "I'm sorry, Little Wolf. Please don't pull away from me."

To my profound relief, she allows me to pull her back against me. I'm hard as stone, my morning erection thick and raging to be freed and to gain access to the woman in my arms.

"I'm so sorry. I haven't woken up with anyone since... The sensation of a warm, female touch in the morning must've transported me back."

"It's fine." I can't see her, but I can hear in her voice that it's not fine. "I shouldn't have been so brash."

I chuckle and draw in a sleepy breath while I stretch. "Wrong. You absolutely should be brash when you're inspired. The burning of our marks won't stop until we consummate our bond. As odd and awkward as it is, the two of us won't be able to fully focus on what's happening in front of us until we come together."

A low feminine groan sounds inches from my face. "I wasn't thinking of taking things that far. I... well, honestly, Dillan spoke to me the other day about me needing to explore my options before I can truly know he's the one. I suppose I got carried away with the idea."

I try to wrap my head around that. "The man you love encouraged you to go and try out other men?"

"His suggestion wasn't gender specific, but because I'm young and a virgin he thought I should at least spend time with more than one person before I'm mated."

What. The. Fuck?

Sooo much in that statement has my head spinning. "Wait. How old are you?"

"I'll be twenty in a few weeks."

Nineteen and a virgin. I ease up on my hold on her and pull my hips back. "Had I known that—"

"Don't," she whispers in a hiss between us. "Please, don't recoil like me being inexperienced changes who I am. If you didn't realize I'm nineteen it's because I'm mature enough that it didn't occur to you."

"Yes... or that we haven't known each other long."

"And about the virgin thing. Doc and I may not have had intercourse, but we've had lots of outercourse and that counts. I know who I am and what I want."

"Or think you do."

The anger that flares in her rich, brown eyes catches me off guard. "Am I to be punished and held at an arm's length because I was raised to believe my body is something to be given to a male only when love is involved?"

Even in the hushed whisper of her words I hear the depth of how much it hurts her to be dismissed. Closing the distance between us, I pull her against me again. I splay my hand up her back and run my fingers into the back of her hair.

I drop my forehead to touch hers. "Keyla, you are amazing. I'm honored you're here with me and you wanted to share yourself with me at whatever level you were hoping for. I'm sorry I backed away. That was about me being unworthy, not you."

"Gah… you sound like him."

"Honestly, it never occurred to me you'd still be a newling. When you returned from an afternoon in the woods with your bear, it seemed obvious what the two of you had been up to. I'm sorry for assuming."

"Stupid enough, I begged him to mate me during our afternoon in the woods. If he had, maybe he'd be here with us and our coupling would look different."

I sigh and stare into the darkness. She's back to the idea of the three of us. "It's not that I want you to suffer or that I have any negative feelings toward your bear."

She chuckles. "Don't you?"

"Okay, I do. That's not him personally, just the fact that another male threatens to take what's mine."

"But why does it have to be either or? What if he's not taking anything but bringing more to both of us? My brother's quint is a spectacular coming together of five lovers. They are so happy and in love. Is it wrong to wish for the same?"

I sigh. "I'm not saying it's wrong. It's simply, what you're suggesting isn't done. Maybe in the badlands you might find things like a threesome coupling but not in our society, and definitely not within the caste of the royal family."

"But I love him. Imagine if Bloom was still alive and the two of you were in love and you and I were bound like this. Could you give her up or would you try to find a way to make it work?"

The mention of Bloom in this context is like a blade piercing my heart. I release my hold on her and roll back. "You don't get to bring her into this. Losing her is my private pain. Maybe I shouldn't have told you."

"No. I'm glad you did. I'm not trying to hurt you. I'm trying to make you understand how I feel."

The stupid thing is I *know* how she feels. If Bloom was alive and the universe wanted me to be with Keyla, I wouldn't be able to choose.

But she's *not* still alive.

"Every day I wish I'd done things differently that horrible morning." I swallow against the emotion clogging my throat. "Maybe she wouldn't have died if she wasn't in my bed. Maybe she wouldn't have died if I hadn't fought our attackers. When things got rough, she fought to get between me and Laryssa's enforcers."

"That was very brave."

"It was. And as much as she meant to me, I knew we could never wed. She was a member of the castle staff. My father wanted me to understand our working-class citizens, he never would've allowed me to marry one. My station deserves..."

"A princess? You think we were soul seared because I'm a royal figurehead?"

"Yes, I do."

When she flops down, I find her hand in the darkness and join our palms so I can think clearly.

"Keyla, I realize you're more than that—I do. You are beautiful and smart and I'm so incredibly thankful you are here. I'm sorry I'm not saying what you want to hear, but we said we'd try to be honest."

"I appreciate that."

Except the mental anguish she's giving off says appreciating it is of little comfort. "Keyla, can we deal with our destiny and our bonding and our escape from Laryssa and all the other things hanging over us without deciding the rest of our life at this moment?"

There's a long, labored pause and then she swallows. "Of course. I'm sorry."

My heart cracks at the sound of her stifled tears thick in her voice. This isn't going as well as it could. Hell, the girl woke me up by palming my cock and now she's crying.

I snuggle her close and draw in the sweet allure of her feminine scent. "I promise, I'll think about your bear and try to find a solution that doesn't break your heart. Don't cry, Little Wolf."

I slide my fingers up the strong column of her neck and brush my thumb over her cheeks, collecting the warm moisture of her tears.

"Please don't cry."

Sadly, it's too late. Whatever hopes I dashed are well and truly broken... I settle us back onto the pallet like we were and urge her to use my shoulder to cry on. Instead of taking me up on it, she shifts forms in my arms and retreats into her wolf.

She gets up on all fours, circles once, and then settles, curled up in a ball. I shift closer to spoon around her and find her front left paw. Sliding it into my palm, I hope the contact will hold the ache of the mating mark at bay enough for us to get back to sleep.

With my free hand, I rub my fingers over the velvety fur of her ears. "Go back to sleep, Little Wolf. Things will look better in the morning. And again... I'm sorry."

Rhylan

We follow the transmission of Creed's tracker chip and arrive in a loft apartment just before four a.m. By the hustle of the investigation team already inside, I'm not sure what we've stumbled into. Leaning to the side at the doorway, I look past the officer on duty and assess what we're dealing with. The place is crawling with night shift enforcers and there's a dead guy on the floor.

"Who's that?" I ask, pointing to the deceased.

The officer on the door checks my credentials and allows us inside. "Meet Riven of Brentwood," another officer says, handing me the deceased guy's identification card. "Dead for almost two hours, I'd say."

"Did anyone see a woman leaving," Doc asks. "Petite, long brown hair… or possibly a white wolf?"

The officer frowns and looks back at me to gauge if he's supposed to answer that. "It's okay. We're looking for someone and have reason to believe she was here."

"You think this is part of a case you're working?"

"I do."

"Which is what, exactly?"

I chuff. I'm certainly not telling a street enforcer Prince Creed escaped the queen's clutches and cut himself free of her security measures. "It's classified."

"Is this what we're tracking?" Brant points to the bloody chip sitting on a stainless-steel tray inside a kitchen trash bin. It's been smashed, but luckily for us, it was still transmitting.

I join them at the table and hold my data scanner over the exposed hardware. "That's it." I grab the chip and pocket it to the horror of the officers in charge.

"You can't come in here and take that. That's evidence. A man was murdered."

I draw my blaster and turn the setting to radiant heat. Next, I fry the biologicals remaining on the operating tools.

The lead officer points to the door and charges us. "Get out of my crime scene, you dragon prick."

"Don't have an aneurysm. There's no crime here. That man killed himself and if it comes down to it, I'll make sure your superiors know it."

The guy looks like he might explode. "You know what happened here, don't you?"

I nod. "I've got a pretty clear idea, yeah. And despite the man dead on the floor, there is no case for you to solve. I've got this. You can close the file and mark it as a crown matter."

"Arrogant prick."

I grin and touch two fingers to my forehead in salute. "Always a pleasure working with the street beat."

CHAPTER THIRTEEN

Keyla

When my eyes open and I realize I won't be getting any more sleep, I stare up at the metal grating above our heads. The underground clan of faery outcasts and unwanteds is starting to stir. The memory of what I did last night looms large between us and I'm mortified.

What was I thinking? I felt up Creed. He was sleeping and I touched his very impressive man parts.

There has to be a morality clause against that in the 'bound but not yet mated' handbook.

Or in the 'you've got a damned boyfriend' book.

Oh, Doc. With the time shift between worlds and everything that happened, I'm not sure how long it's been since he and I spent time together but I miss him.

I want to go back to him, but I need to seek out what is calling us and deal with it first.

"You can't remain in wolf form all day," Creed says, his voice impossibly deep and graveled with sleep. "If this is about last night, I'm sorry if I hurt or embarrassed you. I haven't spoken to a lady for too long. I'll do better. I promise."

He'll do better? I copped a feel and then was about to kiss him. Until he called me Bloom.

A guy calling you by the name of his dead love is a hit to the ego, but I have no right to feel hurt. We just met. We aren't anything to one another.

That lie rings false even in my head.

There is something between us and it's important. The crown of his quadrant hangs in the balance and the unity of the two realms.

"Please, Little Wolf. We must leave, and I'd like to look into your eyes before we're forced to face the world. I messed up last night and I hurt your feelings. I need to know we're still on the same page."

I do as he asks and shift back, flashing my clothes on before I roll back and look at him. "You did nothing wrong. It was my fault. I got carried away with the sensations bombarding. Being on the run with you and having the weight of our situation set in, I swayed beneath the magic of the mating. We said we'd be political allies, not romantic partners and I blurred that line."

Propping his upper body up on his elbow, he frowns. "We blurred that line together and if I'm being honest, there's no way political allies will work."

I stiffen. "Why not? Kotah chose me to be his right hand in running our realm. I'm smart and resourceful and I understand the nuances of powerful and greedy people. I will be a great political ally."

He shakes his head. "Simmer down, Little Wolf. That's not what I was saying."

"Are you still hung up on my age? The number on my birth certification doesn't measure up to what you thought, so my value went down as an ally?"

He shakes his head again, his chest bouncing with silent

laughter. "No. I mean that I find you far too desirable not to want more than a political partnership and with our mating mark forcing the issue, the two of us are destined to be more. There's mating in our future."

My mouth falls open as my cheeks flush hot. "You think I'm desirable?"

"How could I not? I may not have seen you coming, Keyla, but my eyes are open now."

I'm not sure what that means, but honestly, the tunnels are getting busy and privacy is coming to an end.

"So, we're alright?" I ask.

He brings my knuckles to his lips and grins. "We're more than alright. We're partners."

Partners. As silly as it seems, the idea that he considers me on equal footing with him means more to me than any courtship gesture. In the spirit of being equals, I shift our joined hands to my lips and kiss his knuckles. "Partners, then."

We sit for a moment, taking the other in, and then I break the silence. "What's on the agenda first?"

He grins. "First we eat a big breakfast because we have no idea when we'll be able to stop again."

"And then, we follow the buzz in our blood and figure out what's calling us?"

He shakes his head. "I'm torn about that. As much as I want to address our bonding, by now the queen must know I'm missing. I assume she's back and the dragons are out searching for me. Laryssa will hurt my sister to regain control over me. We need to find out where they're holding Honor and free her."

I sit up straight, pull my elastic off my braid, and then brush things out with my fingers. Once I've got the worst of it taken care of, I rebraid it and twist the elastic around the end. "Agreed. You and I are together, and the burning of the call is much less now that we're in your realm. Your sister is the priority. Where do you think we should start?"

He shrugs. "I haven't worked that out yet. The twins will have the city's camera systems scanning for my likeness. I won't be able to take my hood down in the streets and I'm not sure—"

"Majesty." One of the light faeries, Stella, rushes forward with her palm propped in the air and giving off a rainbow of light. "Hurry. Royal enforcers are climbing down the ladders. If you wish to avoid capture, you must leave now."

Doc

"Explain to me again why we're not going down there?" My bear is in full retaliation about being benched by the punk-assed dragon shifter who doesn't even know how to comb his hair out of his eyes.

Sure, I'm as cranky as fuck, but still.

After a long night of eerily empty streets and knocking on doors to force scared people to talk to us, I've had enough. This place is all kinds of messed up and I want Keyla back before something bad happens to her.

Actually, the ship has sailed on that.

Something *worse* then. She's already bound by the universe to a fucking demon dog asshole who's killing people and dragging her into the sewers to sleep.

Yeah, the sewers.

We tracked Keyla from the loft over the illegal gambling hall to the Dornte equivalent of a bus stop and then went to the transportation commission to go through the cameras until we found where they disembarked.

That led us to the row of stores along the road and the security cameras from the crystal shop across the road.

The two of them climbed down this ladder and haven't come topside yet.

"Take it easy, my brother." Brant lays a heavy hand on my shoulder and squeezes it. "We're close. We'll get her back. Calm your bear or you're going to lose control."

"Not gonna happen." My bear's growl rumbles in my chest in a constant warning for people to stay the fuck out of my way. "I need to find her, B."

"I get that. Any minute now. You'll see."

I don't always think of Brant as a comforting force in my life. The guy is too stubborn and reckless for me to have confidence things with him will turn out when he's in charge, but when push comes to shove, the guy is solid.

"That goes for you too, Kotah." He sends his mate a private smile. When we found the lead and tracked them down here, Rhylan had Kotah brought here while we awaited the insurgence team. Apparently, there is a complex maze of tunnels below, and entering from one point would do no good.

This is a four-point tactical breach.

"What about your pack bond." I meet Kotah's worried gaze and shrug. "Can you feel anything? We should be damned close to her."

The guy looks exhausted, but having been down this road with him numerous times during his mating quest, I don't doubt him one bit. He's tougher than he looks and he loves his sister.

Kotah lifts his chin and closes his eyes.

Bears can't track sleuth bonds, but it doesn't surprise me that Kotah and Keyla can sense one another. They are blooded pack and, growing up the way they did, they are as close as two siblings can be.

I watch as Kotah lets his wolf ascend and he raises his nose to the breeze. Standing on the city sidewalk with long strands of his hair escaping his braid and blowing in the breeze, his face turns up toward the early morning sunshine…

"Damn, he looks regal as hell," I whisper.

Brant follows my gaze and grins. "And hot as fuck."

Thankfully, Kotah is either focused enough not to hear, or is ignoring us. Locked in his efforts to connect with his sister, he remains statue-still until his eyes pop wide and he flashes us a look.

When he tilts his head and eases back, he turns and runs off in the opposite direction. I check with Brant and the bear doesn't hesitate for a moment. "Wolf for the win every time, my brother. Hands down, Kotah is the bomb."

We're jogging along the sidewalks of the street when Kotah picks up the pace to run. He takes a right at the first intersection and we're hot on his tail. We tear down the alley after him, the guy's hair flowing in the wind like he's a fucking GQ supermodel.

There aren't many people out yet, the light of the rising sun barely over the horizon of the sleeping city.

"She isn't far," Kotah shouts over his shoulder. "I feel her. They came out another exit. The enforcers are looking in the wrong place."

Brant checks the sightlines, eyeing the rooftops and I know if he sees anything he doesn't like, he will shut this down and take Kotah off the streets. That can't happen.

My bear is barely holding it together.

This has to go our way. There's no other option.

We barrel through another back alley and spook a couple of faeries with green wings. They are searching through the trash and screech as we blaze through.

Brant offers them an apologetic wave.

Another block and we're coming up on a park.

I see her... or, at least, I think it's her. Two people are running hand-in-hand through the trees along a paved pathway. The knife cleaving my heart in two twists as a hard dose of reality hits.

She's not running from him—she's running with him.

Running from us.

The two of them hurdle over a landscaped hedge, their boots propelling them through the public grounds, their cloaks flaring out behind them like they're superheroes or something.

"Nakeyla," Kotah calls out. "Keyla! It's us."

Keyla turns on a dime and yanks Creed to a jarring halt. She looks around and then scurries to the side to duck under the cover of a tree. When we get close enough to stop and talk, she runs at me and launches into the air.

"You came," she breathes against my lips, tears brimming her warm, chocolate eyes. "I'm so sorry. So much has happened but I'm so glad you're here. I love you."

Fuck me. That's good to hear.

Part of me—a small yet very powerful part of me—had pretty much convinced myself it was over and she'd mated and moved on.

I press my nose against her choker and breathe her scent deep into my lungs. My bear lets off a long growl. Her scent has altered. It's not so strong that it says Keyla and Creed mated, but...

"You smell wrong."

Her slender legs slide off my hips and she steps back. "What?"

Kotah cuts in and pulls his sister into his arms. When he eases back, he frowns at me. "It's not *wrong* but it is different. Creed is part of your natural scent now."

Keyla looks at me and shakes her head. "I kissed his cheek one time. That's it... well almost it."

"Forget about that for now," Creed snaps. "We've got to keep moving. Rhy and Vik will be here any minute. They'll drag me back."

I growl, still stuck on her saying 'almost it'. What the fuck does that mean? A kiss to his cheek and what else?

"Kotah won't let them take you." Keyla spins, looking to her brother for reassurance. "There's so much to tell you but the most important thing is that Laryssa is a hateful usurper and holding Creed's sister as leverage to keep him from fighting for his crown. Now that he broke free, we must find her."

Creed nods. "The last time I escaped Laryssa had her guards... hurt her. That can't happen again. Honor is all I have left."

"Not all." Keyla grips his hand, and something passes between them. "You have me now."

Well, that just kicked my nuts up into my throat.

My bear lets off a strangled sound and Keyla looks at me. "You have *us*. We're team Thornebane now, aren't we? The universe wants Creed and I to team up, so that's an endorsement for all of us to get behind him reclaiming his birthright, isn't it, Kotah?"

He dips his chin. "Of course. He is your fated mate and part of our family—"

I catch the shadow swooping in the split-second before the dragon is landing in a run. Its wings remain extended out to catch the drag and slow down. Rhylan goes straight for Creed and Keyla shifts before I've even registered what's happening.

Seriously? She's that sure of this guy that she'd lay down and take on a fucking dragon?

As Brant shifts to join in, Kotah turns to me. "Get them out of here and go somewhere safe. I'll find his sister and we'll make this work. Go."

Kotah flips to wolf and joins Brant and Keyla in the fight. Creed hasn't called his demon dog. Instead, he has a bizarre, silver space blaster and is fiddling with the settings. Once he adjusts things, he weaves around the skirmish and pegs Rhy off a couple of times. The dragon loses steam and the fight drains out of him.

That's my opening to force my bear to get onto team Creed.

"Okay, you two, let's go. Kotah and Brant have this and with all the commotion, reinforcements will be on the way."

Creed meets my gaze and then turns to my white wolf and gets between her and the half-dazed dragon. "Come, Little Wolf. Your bear is joining our cause. Let's go."

Keyla lifts her head, looks at me and I'd swear her wolf smiles. A moment later she's flashing back to her two-legged self and she's grinning from ear to ear.

Racing past me, she grips Creed's hand and the two of them start running off like young lovers. I can't decide if my bear is more hurt or angry but when I look between Kotah and Brant, pinning down the dragon and Keyla and Creed gaining a lead on me, there's only one answer.

Until she says otherwise, I won't give up on her.

CHAPTER FOURTEEN

Rhy

I watch Creed run off with his female and the heavy-hearted bear and I admit, I didn't fight as hard as I could have. Yes, Creed pegged me with stun bolts and the big guy here has the strength of a bulldozer, but even so, I let them win. Why?

"You good, Wolf," Brant says, checking on his mate.

The Wolf King offers the massive male a tender gaze and nods. "Of course. Rhylan didn't have his heart in the fight, did you, Dragon? You weren't trying to win."

I sputter and brush myself off. "Not true. Collecting Creed is my priority."

He points to the three racing through the meandering ribbon of park pathways and shakes his head. "No. You realize you are fighting for the wrong side and are considering what to do about it."

I curse, sitting back on my ass. My head is spinning as if I took a hit in the air and spiraled uncontrollably to the ground. "I don't know what you're talking about."

"I'm talking about the lack of bloodshed or broken bones. You wanted Creed to retain his freedom."

Smart man. "I see your lips moving, King, but I don't hear you saying anything."

The male dips his chin. "Then, let me be clearer. My sister is in the mix now. Her destined place is at the side of Prince Creed. There is nothing I won't do to ensure she lives a safe and happy life, including removing anyone who means to do them harm from the playing field."

"That's not me."

"No, but it was obvious in the first moments of our first encounter Laryssa is a leader who uses force and fear. She won't stand for Creed gaining support and will act against Keyla. That won't happen. That woman's reign is ending. It's time for you to reevaluate your position."

I growl and exhale. I've never explained to anyone the truth of what binds Vik and me into her service but he's right, I either betray my honor or my duty. "It's not that simple."

"What complicates it?"

It's none of his business but after seeing how people rally around him and his sister, I admit, I'd rather deal with them than Laryssa. Maybe he can help us.

Deciding to not make a decision, either way, I give him half the story. "My brother and I were offered to serve Laryssa in a lose-lose order from our brood alpha, Shadowcaster. The asshole ruined our family name and we're honor-bound—"

"—Incoming." Brant points into the brilliance of the rising sun and I follow his scowl.

Vikarus flies over the cluster of trees we're hidden beneath and descends to pluck Creed from the ground.

The extraction is a lightning strike and there's no possible defense. The three of us race to close the distance, our arms pumping as our boots thunder against the manicured ground. There's no chance of stopping this.

My twin has the prince in his clutches and is arching in the morning sky to return to the castle.

"Go," Kotah shouts throwing his hand into the air. "Catch him and bring them down."

"I can't." I let off a long-suffering groan. "Creed shot me with enough electrical disruption to keep me grounded for hours. I can't fly."

By the time the three of us reach Doc and Keyla, Vik is a dark speck in the sky.

"Creed!" Keyla sends me a wide-eyed look of terror. "Stop this. Bring him back. Please! I know you care about him."

I don't know what she thinks she knows but that's a mystery for another moment. I pull out my security tablet and type him an emergency message.

Vik! Don't return Creed to the castle. Circumstances have changed. Call me.

I send the message and then point toward the nearest main street. "All we can do is try to get there before things go to hell. Come on."

The five of us sprint across the park grounds and I wave down an unmanned shuttle for hire. I scan my credentials into the nav screen and program our destination. "Thornebane Castle. Maximum speed."

Keyla

I clutch the upholstered seat of the shuttle, staring out the front windshield, tears blurring my vision. This can't be happening. We were almost to safety—both the men in my life with me. And now—

"What will she do to him?" I ask, swallowing past the lump in my throat. "What will she do to his sister?"

Rhylan swivels his front seat around to face the back seat. "I sent a message to Vik. Everything depends on whether he gets it in time."

"He won't get it before he lands at the castle," Brant says. "Unless you dragons have a pocket in your hip scale and can check your messages with your talons."

Rhy frowns and pulls out a security tablet like the one I have in my bag. "No. You're right. No matter how this plays out, Creed will be returned to the castle."

"What about his sister?" Kotah asks. "From the gut-wrenching guilt and fury Creed gave off when he spoke of what Laryssa's guards did to her the last time he escaped, she has to be a priority. We can help secure Creed but there's no one to safeguard her."

"That's true, but that will only be necessary if Laryssa knows he escaped and has unlocked his powers. If she believes he simply took his female home—"

"*Nakeyla.*" Doc growls and leans forward in his seat. He's not buckled in, so he could easily make this trip to the castle very dangerous. "Don't refer to her as 'his female'. It's offensive. She has a name and it's Nakeyla Northwood or the Prime Princess."

I roll my eyes and rub at the ache in my palm.

His bear is wound up but I don't need him getting bent out of shape defending me.

Rhy dips his chin but can barely meet my gaze. Then again with the mop of blond tangles, covering his face, how can I tell? "My apologies. If Laryssa believes Creed and the princess accompanied the king and his mates to explore the castle and the city, she won't want to stir up trouble. In that case, Honor is in no immediate danger."

"We still need to locate her and secure her well-being," I say. "The safety of her and their mother is the only reason he hasn't moved on Laryssa to reclaim his throne. Now that he knows his mother is dead—"

"When did he find that out?" Brant asks. "You say that like it's a new development."

"It's new that he knows but not new that she passed. When Creed scanned Rhylan's mind during our escape from the encampment, he found out."

Rhy sinks forward and props his elbows on his knees. "I hated that I couldn't tell him. It was a coward's tactic on Laryssa's part and he deserved better."

I hiss and shake my hand out. The attempt does nothing to alleviate the growing discomfort, so I ball my fist. "No argument, but still you lied to him. That choice was yours to make and you went along with her."

Rhy curses and drops his face into his palms. He recovers quickly and rakes his fingers over his forehead.

It's the first time I've seen the man's face and I'm dumbstruck. Dazzled. Rhylan is stunning. I study his face and it's as if each plane of his brow, cheekbone, and jaw have been chiseled by the Norse gods.

"He must be devastated." The weight in his tone indicates that he too is devastated. Is his heartache for a lover learning terrible news? Or is he upset Creed found out through him and now knows he kept it a secret?

"Hurt and betrayed were the exact words he used," I add, to let him know what he's facing.

He drops his gaze and his hair falls forward and cuts off any chance of reading his expressions.

"You knew his mother died and kept it from him. That is a difficult position to be in." Kotah has a way of stating things without judgment. It's one of the things I love most about confiding in him.

Kotah is a safe place—for me, and others as well. It will serve him well to become an amazing ruler.

"Being duty-bound is a difficult thing. Your brood alpha did you and your brother a disservice to put you in the position he did."

Rhy shrugs. "That doesn't change much in the end though, does it?"

My brother and Rhy continue to discuss the prickly workings of brood politics, but the lava shooting up my arm keeps me from following the discussion.

The fire of the mating brand is leaching its way up my arm and into my shoulder. The pain is intense and it's all I can do not to scream out. I'm beginning to think that not only is the branding burn time-sensitive but it's also proximity sensitive.

The two of us have stayed separated this long before but it never hurt a fraction as bad as it does now.

I grip my wrist and clench my eyes shut.

The male chatter stops. I feel what's meant to be the soothing touch of my bear on my forearms but it's not soothing at all—it's excruciating.

Crying out, I recoil. I open my eyes in time to see the agony in Dillan's hazel eyes.

"I'm sorry." I push back and away from them. "I didn't mean to react like that."

"What did I do, babe? I smell your pain. What's happening?"

It takes everything I have to uncurl my fingers and show them my palm. "It's burning worse than ever."

"He branded you?" Doc shouts, glaring at my palm. "That motherfucking demon dog—"

"Creed didn't do that," Rhy shouts back. "The brand is part of the searing. Why do you think they never let go of one another? They can't be parted until their union is consummated."

Kotah drops to his knees before me, looking horrified. "You should've told us, sister mine."

"It was already too late," I gasp, pulling up my knees and

wrapping myself in a ball. "Vik already flew away and we're headed to find him."

"Well I hope he suffers from this too, and it's not just her," Doc says.

"Why would you say that?" I brush at the tears burning down my cheeks and glare. "This searing happened to him too. He's been kind and caring to me and you're being a jerk. Stop badmouthing him."

Before he can respond, Kotah is there. He touches my leg tentatively and then nods. "I thought as much. I'm no threat to your mating bond. Your body reacted negatively to Doc because he is. Here, let me help you."

I hadn't realized the shuttle stopped until Kotah lifts me out of my seat and curls me against his chest. Wildlings are very strong. I weigh nothing in his arms but still, if I could manage to walk on my own, I would.

Instead, I curl up like a child in his arms and sob against Kotah's chest. "It hurts so bad."

There's a lot of commotion as we follow Rhylan into the staff entrance of the castle and begin to weave our way through the private corridors. My attention is fractured but I catch glimpses of soaring arches and grand finishes and curious gazes as we make our way.

The fire is so intense now, I'm certain I'll join Calli as the second female wildling to burst into flames. It's beyond anything I can talk myself out of.

It's beyond anything I could've imagined.

My wolf claws at my insides, trying to escape. She's panicked and feral. I tip my head back and we howl to the gods above. The cry echoes from all around, my soul shattering into crystals of agony.

The howl continues long past the point of needing breath and my world begins to darken.

Men are shouting and I realize Kotah is in a full run.

Yes. Hurry. Find my mate.

I try to hang on. Kotah will fix this.

If there is one thing in life my wolf and I know to the depths of our soul, it's that Kotah will always make things right.

Except, I can't hold on any longer. The world is slipping away and my blood is boiling in my veins.

Creed

I sense the brush of her mind from where I've retreated. I'm locked in the deepest recess of my soul, trapped in the knowledge that once again the woman in my life is dying and there's nothing I can do to get to her in time.

To save her.

To keep her for myself.

I never imagined the pain of losing Bloom could be over-shadowed, but this is more—much more.

Losing Bloom struck me in my heart but this...

Keyla's energy is ingrained in my cells, my soul, my very being. My need to touch her is transcendent. I can't move. I can't breathe. I can't live.

Reaching out, I try to find her again. Did I really feel her the first time or was it pain-induced cruelty perpetrated by my psyche?

I search, my heart about to char and crumble into brittle black dust...

She's here.

I open my eyes as people burst into my chambers. Rhy searches the bed and the rest of the room before finding me curled up on the floor. Rushing forward, he grabs under my shoulders.

I scream with more breath than I can spare.

"Don't touch him," Kotah shouts, racing forward and lying Keyla's too still form against me.

Keyla. I scramble to find her hand and force her fingers to open. Palm to palm I drop my forehead to rest against her and I wait and cry and pray it's not too late.

Come to me, Little Wolf. The pain is over. Come to me and we'll face this together.

~

Doc

How do you fight something like that? Part of me hoped Creed *had* mind-warped Keyla somehow and that's why she left me behind. Then I figured it was her commitment to the bonding and the destiny they're supposed to unfold together for this realm. But watching them the moment he pulled her into his arms and her body finally relaxed after almost thirty minutes of torture...

It's nothing like that.

The two of them are a couple or will be. They might not have worked out the kinks yet, but they are a 'they'.

My legs threaten to give out and I stumble back and assplant into the chair behind me. The crashing brings Creed's attention to me. Our gazes lock for a long while and then he musters up the strength to get himself and Keyla off the polished floor of his royal suite.

The rooms are darkly masculine, of course—the heir to the Dornte throne having an image of manly grace to live up to—and the focal point of the main bed chamber is the massive four-poster he uses as a bed.

This is the kind of place Nakeyla Northwood deserves. She can slum it in jeans and a knit sweater but she belongs in diamonds and gowns.

He can give her that.

The Fates have spoken.

Now, if I can just pull myself together enough to leave them to it.

Moving with the speed and strength of the walking dead, Creed shuffles across the floor and sets Keyla in his bed. "Thank you for reuniting us. If it had been longer, without a doubt, neither of us would've survived."

"But she will," Kotah says, his words more imperial decree than an actual question.

Creed settles her still form as close to the center of the mattress as he can. Then, he props the pillows and climbs up himself. When he settles beside her, he takes her hand and closes his eyes as if touching her is the balm to his very soul. "She will but we both need time to recover. What of my sister?"

Kotah places his fist over his heart. "The dragon and I will assess the situation and take action on your behalf. Take the time you need with my sister and I will work to safeguard yours. I do so swear."

"Thank you. Please keep me apprised." Creed extends a hand and Kotah accepts it and they seal the deal. After Kotah's recent bonding I understand why he's pro-Creed, but it still stings.

With their pledge of sister care made, Kotah nods to Brant and the two of them head for the door.

I force myself to my feet and when I'm sure my legs will support me, begin my exit.

"Stay, Bear." Creed's obsidian gaze pierces me with emotions I can't even begin to guess. "If you will."

I lift my chin to Brant's quizzical look and shrug. "I'll hear him out and catch up with you later."

Rhylan glances back as if he has something to say to the prince but the guy shakes his head and waves him off. "Get the fuck out. Find your asshole brother and see how much damage the two of you have done."

Something passes between them and then the dragon twin takes his leave.

I wait until the latch of the door clicks and then widen my stance and clasp my hands at my back. Old habits and all that. When life gets impossible, falling back on the rote training helps hold the pieces together.

"She loves you."

I meet the man's gaze and nod.

"She says you love her and intended to mate her."

I'm not sure what kind of cruelty this is, but it's already a train wreck and I can't look away. "I've thought of little else for months."

"And yet you held back and suggested she broaden her understanding of other men first?"

Fuck me. Is that what this is about? He wants to take me up on that asinine idea. I take it back. For reals. "I was stupid. I should've gone with my bear's instinct and claimed her when she agreed to be my mate."

"Why didn't you?"

I hiss, the air filling with the warning of my bear's last straw being tested. "This is none of your business."

"It is. Keyla wants to expand our union to include you. She admires the relationship her brother has with his mates and thought it might be an option so the two of you could continue."

Um, pardon? My cognitive brain connections start flicking on and off like faulty Christmas lights. Did she pitch him us as a throuple? "But what about destiny and the whole mirrored soul thing?"

"If you had mated her that afternoon by the river, there would be nothing for me to decide. The two of us would simply have to come to an agreement."

"But I didn't. So, you don't."

"But if you had," he says letting that thought hang in the air, "could you live with an arrangement like that?"

My first instinct is to throw my arms up in the air and yell 'Yes. Hells yes. A thousand times, yes'. I don't. He holds all the power and I have to give it the consideration it deserves. "Are we talking about her and I alone and you and her alone or more than that?"

"You tell me. Matings like this aren't done or accepted in this realm, but you two aren't from this realm and I'm wondering if that gives me leeway. Many fae species participate in group events and keep multiple lovers but they aren't bound by the titles of mated or married. I'm trying to get a sense of what we could be."

I study him and let my bear weigh in. "My first reaction is that I would do anything to be with Keyla. That you're even entertaining the idea of allowing us to mate is more than… well, you've blown my mind."

"It's not about me. Keyla is mine to care for. As a soldier and a medic, you offer skills we might need. As a man, you offer her the happiness she has her heart set on. I need to understand how it would work."

I step closer and grip the footboard. Looking at the two of them curled together makes my bear crazy but knowing their contact keeps her alive helps.

"Bears are pack animals and might be considered promiscuous by your standards. We tend to find pleasure in whatever package it comes in. I've enjoyed sexual experiences with men and women. I've participated in those group events you mentioned, and I have no hang-ups or inhibitions."

"We have that much in common."

"And I admit, looking at you, I see the physical appeal. You're a good-looking guy and you seem decent."

He dips his chin. "As do you."

"The three of us is a possibility but beyond that, I can't comment. I spent the past two days hating and envying you. Swordplay never crossed my mind."

His mouth quirks up at the side in a crooked smirk. "Since Keyla brought it up, swordplay *has* crossed my mind and I think we'd both enjoy it."

Holy fuck. His deep, graveled voice drops an octave and sends a zing of dark and dirty desire right to my cock. Fuck me, I think we would enjoy it.

Creed slides down the bed, pulling a couple of pillows out from under his head, and tosses them along the headboard. "Grab the coverlet there and tuck us in. We'll discuss it after Keyla and I have a chance to recover."

Is this really happening? I spot the blanket in question and stride over grab it. Shaking the thing out, I cover Creed and Keyla and then round the bed to what essentially might be 'my side'.

Hells to the yes. This could work. Fuck. If it means I get to keep Keyla, I'll make it work.

I climb onto the mattress and pull the cover over me.

"Please don't touch her." He holds out his hand to stop me from rolling onto my side and snuggling tight to Keyla. "You won't be able to touch her until we have consummated our union."

My bear roars at the idea of him taking her virginity from me, but there's nothing to be done about that. Soul seared trumps I should've mated her when I could have.

Nothing will be settled until Keyla weighs in, but if this was her idea, I have to believe that's a formality. Reaching over her still form, I hold my knuckles up for a bump. "Thank you. I was in real danger of losing my soul there for a bit."

I'm not sure if Creed doesn't know what to do with a knuckle bump or he wants to ad-lib, but he spreads his fingers and laces his hand with mine.

The connection sends tingles of warmth dancing across my skin, his powers responding to mine. That's never happened to me with a dude before but hey, that's a good sign for things to come, right?

"You are welcome, Bear. The universe gave me Keyla to take care of. I will live and die making every effort to ensure she has everything she needs. She made it clear she needs you."

There doesn't seem to be resentment or hostility in those words and I'm still too blown away to come up with a suave response. There's too much whirling around inside me to express what this means.

When my eyes glass up, I bow out of the whole thing and simply close my eyes. Life kicks you in the ass when you least expect it.

Damn. Keyla will lose her mind when she wakes up.

CHAPTER FIFTEEN

Rhy

"What the slecking hell is going on?" Vik meets us head-on as I escort the Wolf King and his bear mate out of the prince's private quarters.

I let the anguish of my day loose and give my twin a raw-throated growl. "How about we discuss this in private. We've been up all night and I'm sure we'd all feel better if we could get a few hours of sleep."

"I'm sure," Kotah says, "but I made a promise to your prince."

Gods, give me strength. "Vik, what does the queen know about what happened?"

"Know or suspect?"

"Does she know Creed escaped? Will there be backlash for Honor?"

Vik glares and then looks at the Wolf King. "What happened to us discussing things in private?"

"Creed told his mate everything. His mate told her family. There's no sense trying to deny it." In truth, it was me who told them, but why volunteer that?

Vik chews on that for a moment and then shrugs. "Queen Laryssa is annoyed and suspicious but since he's here and all eyes are on her, she'll tamp down her suspicions. No, I don't think she has any designs on bringing Honor into it."

Small miracles.

I point the way to the guest suites within Creed's quarters and smile. "I'll start working on things we discussed and we can revisit once everyone has had a chance to recharge."

I'm not sure if my need to speak to my twin outweighs my pride in my work, but I can't be bothered to escort them. "This floor of this section of the castle is all part of the original Royal Wing and therefore Creed's quarters. There are guards to keep people out of this wing, so we pretty much have the run of the floor. I'm directly across the hall here. Vik is in that suite, there. And you two can take The Auburn Suite there. Make yourself at home."

"Good enough," Brant says. "We'll check back when we're rested up and need to find the dining room."

I nod. "I'll have something sent up in the meantime. If they knock and you don't answer, I'll instruct them to leave the cart outside the door."

"That works." The two males walk off, eager to lay their heads down and I envy them.

I step across the hall and scan my hand for entry into my suite. "I'm really, slecking tired, Vik, so let's make this quick. Tell me what you said to Laryssa. What does she know?"

"It's safe to say finding you and Creed gone raised some major flags. Using the excuse that we wanted to let her sleep wasn't well received."

I unbutton my shirt and let it drop to the carpet. "I didn't expect it would be. Does she suspect he escaped under our watch?"

"I don't know. She didn't kill me, and she didn't threaten to kill you, so there's that. Maybe there were too many potential problems with Kotah's mates watching her, I don't know."

Unbuckling my weapon's belt, I set it on my table and unbuckle my boots. "But she never mentioned pulling Honor into it?"

"No. Why were they asking about Honor?"

"Because Creed's freaked out that his solo excursion will cause another round of violence against his sister and the Wolf King is determined to help ensure she's safe. Like it or not, the opening of the rift has now put us on the unpopular side of things. We'll have to play this just right if we want to survive."

"What is there to play? We're bound to back Queen Laryssa. If we fail, Mom and the Silverwing name will suffer more than they already have."

Vik isn't one to envision the long-game strategy.

He sees things happening in real-time and reacts.

I strip off my pants and crawl into my unmade bed. Pulling the covers over me, I close off the world. "One good thing is Laryssa will be paranoid about the Wolf King and his mates seeing the cracks in her rule. She'll be cautious about making overt moves until they leave."

Vik smirks. "Then maybe we can convince them to move into the castle. If they never leave, we might get some peace in our lives."

I chuckle. "I'll settle for a few hours of sleep."

Vik waves that away. "I told you my side of the updates. Now you tell me what the hell happened here. Where were you? Why did you send me that text? Why wouldn't I bring Creed back?"

There's no way I'll get any sleep until this is over, so I start at the beginning. "Creed and his mate are being called by some unseen force related to their searing. They got back to the portal hub, made it across town, removed his tracking chip, had some kind of altercation with a member of his father's council."

"I heard about that. An enforcer complained one of the

queen's dragons ruined his crime scene. I was questioned about it, but I wasn't even in the realm."

"Too bad, so sad. I took care of it. So, anyway, Creed killed him, hid in the park tunnels overnight, and then ran when we flushed the tunnels. You swooped down during their escape and now you're all caught up."

"And, where were you?"

"When?"

"When they escaped the tunnels."

"In pursuit, about three hundred feet behind them under the trees in the park."

"I didn't see you."

I can't say I was standing under a tree watching them run away. Vik and I are tight but he's way too by the book to support dereliction of duty. "You came in from over the Lichenze Tower, plucked Creed off the park grounds, and banked over the Markdom Cathedral before beating your wings back here."

I yawn, watching him retrace my words. "Okay, so you were there. Why didn't you shift and capture him?"

"Slecking hell, Vik, I'm *tired*. He stun-blasted me like five times as I went after him. I couldn't get air."

He purses his lips, but I think he's finally running out of steam.

"I need to sleep, my brother. Can we be done?"

"One more. Why did you message me not to bring him back here? You said things had changed. What does that mean?"

I groan and my dragon lets him hear how done we are with this conversation. "It means the woman Creed is bonded to is the sister of the Wolf King. We can't treat Creed like a prisoner anymore. You swept him up and separated them. They both nearly died. We don't know enough about soul searing to proceed as if things haven't changed. We have to be smart."

He nods. "I heard her wolf howling as they brought her in. It was eerie. The haunted pitch of that call unnerved my dragon."

I nod. "The two of them are bound. They can't be separated. What do you think the Wolf King will do if we kill their princess the first day she arrives?"

Vik lets off a long sigh. "It was a close call but to be fair, I didn't have all the facts."

"Fair enough. No more close calls, Vik. We need to play nice and that means we escort Creed and Keyla as they investigate their calling. We smile and help the Wolf King and it would go a long way with them if we give them some news on the whereabouts of Honor."

He screws up his face. "And betray Laryssa? Are you insane? If she doesn't kill us, Shadowcaster will."

I pull a pillow over my face and scream. Since that doesn't actually solve anything, I give my brother a glare. "I said 'play' nice asshole not betray our bond and get ourselves killed."

"Oh, okay, good."

"Now get out of my suite and see what you can find out about Honor. And for gods' sake, do it covertly. Don't let anyone know we're asking around or why. Do you think you can manage that?"

"I got it. There's no need to be such a derisive dick. Get some sleep. You're miserable."

I throw my pillow at him, catching him in the back of the head as he gets to the door.

When he's finally gone, I take a deep breath and close my eyes. I need sleep. I need to escape reality for a bit and stop seeing the betrayal in Creed's gaze as he ordered me out of his bedroom.

Get the fuck out.

Yeah, that hurt.

Keyla

The searing kiss of summer sun on naked skin has me groaning and stretching on the mossy bank of the grotto. Being naked in the outdoors is highly erotic and the warmth of the sun makes it that much more enjoyable. I open my eyes and let my right leg dip down beneath the cool turquoise water of the waterfall pool.

"Where have you brought us, Little Wolf?"

I follow the husky call of Creed's voice to where he moves to stand over me. He's naked except for a pair of black leather sex shorts with silver buckles across the front. His body is taut, his stance relaxed, his silver hair hanging down his chest to toy with the platinum ring through his nipple.

If this wasn't a dream, I might be embarrassed that I dressed him in something so sexually aggressive but it is a dream, so hey, might as well enjoy the view.

Embrace the creative mind, right?

My wolf is an alpha predator and Creed is a part of us now. He is mine.

I inventory the lines of navy blue inking that run from the muscled round of his right shoulder down the plane of his pectoral, over the rippled ridges of his six-pack to the dip in his hip that veers toward his cock.

I bite my lip and point to his erection pushing at those buckles and hold up my finger. "I'll come back to you in a moment. Don't go anywhere."

Creed's throaty chuckle does sinful things to me.

But first, the tattoo. I saw a glimpse of it in the cabin when I woke the other night but everything was so new and jumbled, I didn't get a chance to enjoy it.

"What does this mean?"

Creed steps closer and I watch the pinch and release of his stomach muscles as he approaches. "It's a record of the lineage of my family written in the old language of my ancestral people. It tells the story of the crown guardians—the Amberloq warriors—and how they became the guardians of the Dornte throne."

"It's beautiful."

"Thank you. As is yours." He taps a finger against his Adam's apple and lifts his chin to show me his neck. The action surely means more to me than it does to him. Exposing your neck to a predator is an act of trust and submission.

I can't imagine I've earned his trust thoroughly enough to gain his submission. Still, it's a heady thought.

"I've never seen ink glitter like that before," he says.

I trace my fingers over my choker. I rarely think about it. It just is. "It's infused with magic."

His smile tells me he already knew that. I draw a deep breath and swing my foot in gentle circles in the water of the grotto pool. "This is a lovely dream. It's vibrant and sexy and feels real."

"It is real. In a fashion."

"What do you mean?"

"I mean the two of us are physically exhausted and sleeping in my bed at the castle but I am a mind fae—a powerful one at that. I have the ability to dreamwalk and when I knocked, your mind was more than welcoming to let me in."

"Well, that's embarrassing." I clap my legs closed and shift to sit up. My cheeks flare with heat.

Creed holds out his palms and shakes his head. "Please, don't feel that way."

"Dreams are one thing—I've been so sexually charged lately I like the sexy dreams. If this is real, or sort of real, it's too much. I don't want to hurt Doc."

"Then you don't need to worry. Your bear and I spoke and I invited him to join our mating."

"You what?" I leap to my feet and search his expression for

any hint that he's joking or lying or that I misunderstood. "I can mate him? You don't mind?"

"Of course, I do. I am a dominant male and the universe gave you to me. It's a strike to my ego that you still choose the bear but I understand the depth of your love for him. I think inviting him to join us makes sense for your safety, your happiness, and if we're being forthcoming, I think it will be fun sexually too."

I launch forward and hug him tight, our bare chests crushed so tightly together we're practically one. The contact is magical and the scent of his arousal is so powerful it makes me dizzy.

"Thank you."

I run my fingers along his chiseled jaw and into his hair. "Thank you."

Pushing up onto my tip-toes I meet his mouth with mine and kiss him with everything I have. He's giving me the ultimate gift—the two men I want.

Before I get too carried away, I slow the kiss. My wolf growls, her territorial rumble vibrating in my chest between us.

I ease back, nip his lip, and tug. "Thank you."

His eyes aren't the black coal or pearl opulence of his curse. The whites are still iridescent opal but he has beautiful purple irises surrounding his pupils. They are stunning and dancing with hunger.

"Did Dillan give us his blessing?"

Creed's brow arches as a smirk warms his face. "I don't suppose any man would. The fact is, the searing won't allow him to touch you until we've accepted our mating. I realize you offered your body to him... so I thought this was our best option. You and I can come together like this and then you and he can make love on the physical plane."

"Will this satisfy the searing so he can touch me?"

"Yes. It *is* real. It's simply on the mental plane. A great deal of the pleasure of sex is mental over physical already. The mind is a powerful sexual organ."

I close my eyes as I take stock of how sharp and sensual the impulses are between us. I like mind sex.

"Will this work for you if the two of us consummate our mating here like this?"

I read the hopeful light in those stunning purple eyes and I fall for him a little more. When Doc touched me in the shuttle it was excruciating. I can be like this with Creed and then Doc will still be my first... sort of.

Honestly, Doc has been my first for everything I've done sexually. Maybe it's nice Creed gets this much.

I step back and raise my palm, letting the warmth of the sun wash over me. This will change everything. The universe has given us little choice, but to accept him locks in a different future to any I planned.

In the reflection of the water's surface I study the image of the two of us together. Nothing about this feels wrong. Whatever magical purpose is playing out, being his queen and accepting this future is the right choice.

"I can't think of a better way."

He winks and connects our brands, lacing his fingers with mine. The mark isn't burning here but the contact is just as pleasureful as it is in the physical world.

I groan as the connection hits me right between the legs. His gaze drops to the stiff tips of my nipple. Heat rushes to my core and in an instant, I'm damp and wracked with desire.

"There are so many things I need. Be a prince, will you, and take those shorts off."

He chuckles. With slow, teasing movements, he undoes the first of the three buckles. "I was surprised you dressed me in this. What does the beloved Prime Princess of the Human Realm know of bondage leathers?"

I waggle my brow and resume my place on the mossy lip of the grotto to watch the show. Rolling onto my side, I prop my head up with my hand and give him something to look at too.

"When Kotah renovated a part of the palace for him and his mates, he and Hawk ordered a lot of private equipment and apparel for their quint to enjoy. I received the order."

He chuckles and moves down to the next buckle. "Your brother had you handle his fetish delivery?"

"Oh, no. He would be mortified if he knew I did. It was all boxed up very discreetly, but when I signed the manifest, I noticed the company name and curiosity got the better of me. I looked up a few of the items. I may have even wondered about a few."

He drops his fingers to the last buckle and arches a brow. "And does the visual meet your expectations?"

I bite my bottom lip and grin. "Oh, yeah. You look good in leather and buckles."

"You surprise me at every turn, Nakeyla."

I lean back and stretch, letting my knees fall open the way Doc likes. "And is it a good surprise?"

"The best kind." When the leather bottoms fall to the mossy ground, he stands before me and lifts his hands from his sides. "What about you. Are you pleased with what you're getting?"

As much as I'd love to be suave and say something alluring and sexy I giggle and stomp my bare feet against the ground. "Is it wrong to want to growl? I look at you and my animal ascends so strongly I just want to growl."

He barks a laugh. "Then growl away, Little Wolf. Let me hear your wolf's approval."

I let my wolf voice her approval. Staring might not be polite, but I don't want to ever look away. "You're so smooth. Mind fae don't have body hair?"

"Only on the top of my head. Is that good or bad?"

"Oh, on you, it's great. No judgment either way but yeah... it's super sexy on you." I'm still staring, and it's becoming awkward.

Must. Stop. Staring.

To end the torture, I roll off the edge of the bank and into the warm water of the grotto's limestone pool. It's deep enough by the edge that when I breach the surface and stand, the water comes to my waist. "Welcome to my favorite place in the world."

Creed hops down into the water beside me and then dunks himself. When he straightens, he runs his hands over his head and the water glistens on his skin like an erotic movie. With every step he takes to close the distance between us, my heart races a little faster.

Glancing down at the crystal clear water, he smiles at the colorful fishes darting around our legs. "It's incredible here. Where is your favorite place in the world?"

"Remember when I told you my parents left us on pack lands to be raised out of sight?"

He searches the area around us and smiles. "This versus life in a palace? I think you got the better end of that arrangement."

"You're not wrong. Although, knowing we'd been discarded by our parents wasn't great."

He steps in tight to me and wraps his arm across the small of my back. "Forgive me. I didn't mean that."

I reach up and link my hands behind his neck. "It's fine. Kotah and I came to terms with it long ago and you're right. Being raised here molded who we are."

He grins and runs the backs of his fingers down the outside of my breast. "I look forward to getting to know who you are. Ours may not be a traditional route to a union but who are we to question the universe?"

I giggle. "Says the naked man about to have sex. All we've done for a day and a half is question the universe."

He grins. "That's true. Although, you have certainly seemed more sure of things from the start."

"Only because I've been living this with my brother for months. It's been amazing to see their lives unfold. From the moment it happened to us, my only point of contention was losing Dillan. Now that you've fixed that, I couldn't be more excited."

"Then let's see what unfolds."

I press my branded palm to the hard plane of his chest. "I know a large part of your heart is still wounded, but that's alright. I'm here for you. I want you to be happy, however that looks."

He nods. "And I, you. In that vein, because you have little experience, things we do might be new for you. Tell me if I make a misstep or there's something you don't like. This will only be truly enjoyable for both of us if we are frank and honest."

I skim my hand down his wet chest and under the surface of the water to brush his impressive cock. "Then I'll tell you one thing now. Don't princess me. Doc can't seem to stop treating me like I'm a precious gem. I've asked him to pin me down and consume me but he insists on pampering me. Don't mistake inexperience for me being fragile. I'm not. My wolf is hungry."

He laughs again and the sound is deep and sensual. "The best kind of surprise. Alright, I'll leave the pampering to your bear and I'll take you hard and dirty."

I pump my fist in the air. "Yes. Exactly what I wanted to hear."

CHAPTER SIXTEEN

Creed

Keyla is hilarious and filled with so much hopeful energy I can't help but be swept away. Unbridled passions. I realize she and her bear have been both sensual and sexual but there is something I can give her he hasn't or won't. Stupid fool.

Claiming her as an equal force in the pairing.

Reaching under her arms, I grip her sides and lift her to sit on the lip of the grotto wall. "Legs over my shoulders and lean back."

"Yes, sir." She leans back on her elbows and stretches her legs over my shoulders so my head is trapped between her legs. Her eyes glitter with mischief as she bites her bottom lip and watches.

She truly isn't like any female I've ever met.

Maybe it's because she's from another realm or because she was raised as a royal and isn't intimidated by me or my position. Whatever the reason, I love how confident she is. If anything, her sureness intimidates me.

A little.

Never a man to shy away from a challenge, I dip my head down to take her by mouth. I pause to give us both a moment to anticipate what comes next.

In the beat of hesitation, I absorb the view from her core. It's a glorious journey up the glistening copper skin of her body, over the soft curls of hair on her mons, across the flat plane of her belly, over the swells of her lush breasts to lock with her gaze.

She nips her lip, smiling down at me.

"You are breathtaking, Nakeyla. I'm honored you trust me with your body and honored you are mine."

I leave that in the air between us and seal my lips over hers. She shudders as I begin to inventory all her moist nooks. Her skin is silk against my lips, her natural feminine flavor a balm to my suffering.

My female. My sweet and sexy female,

I've missed this. Fucking Rhy is about anger and control. This is so much more.

I sweep my tongue, laving her nerves and bringing her need forward. She arches her hips, pressing firmly against my mouth, demanding more. So wound up. How could that fool have a woman like this, as horny as this, and leave her unsated?

It's a crime.

It's also his loss because I am going to work her over so thoroughly our first time will be seared into her mind for eternity.

As I shift and nuzzle, the water of the grotto rises and falls against my skin. This place is magical. I'm so incredibly grateful our first time is in this oasis.

I take my time learning her body and preferences. After the chaotic pace of the past few days, this is heavenly. No wonder the bear lost his mind when he thought he was losing her.

She's hungry... playful... utterly entrancing.

Keyla's thighs tighten against my jaw and I sense her release nearing. I could open up her mind completely so our thoughts and sensations merge but I want to wait.

That's a surprise for when I'm pounding inside her and she's finally getting what she's wanted.

Instead, I work my fingers into the mix. If Doc's pampering her like a princess, I bet he's never played with her ass. I slide my thumb through her channel and then press against the resistance of her back entrance.

"Oh," she gasps, jolting against my mouth as if I've shocked her with an electrical charge. "Oh, that's... interesting."

I play a moment, moistening the tight gathering of flesh before I thrust my thumb inside.

Her wolf growls. Somehow, I understand the tone of her animal. There's a little confusion over the sensation but it's all good. Hard and dirty. You asked and I will deliver.

"Oh, that's nice... crazy nice."

For two years I've been without this kind of connection—physical and mental.

For two years I've suffered, alone in my mind, isolated from the psychic energy that fuels my gift.

Her wolf lets off another growl as she pushes back on my thumb and forces the penetration deeper. My cock pulses beneath the tropical waters, hard and thick.

Fuck, I need inside her.

Keyla stiffens and shatters, her legs clamping my ears as she arcs back and cries out my name. She's a vocal thing. I grin. Good. I want her voice to carry through the halls of the Dornte castle and get everyone talking.

When the waves of her orgasm settle, I withdraw my thumb, rinse off in the water, and then hop up to the mossy ground to claim my mate.

I lay over her, settling my torso in the cradle of her hips. Reaching forward, I claim her mouth. Keyla meets my kiss with a level of sexual aggression I love. She forces her tongue through the seam of my lips and challenges my tongue to a sexy duel.

I fight not to chuckle.

She's a wild one, my Little Wolf.

We kiss like horny teenagers for a bit and then she pulls back gasping. "A good start?"

She grins. "A great start, thank you."

"You said no pampering. You want hard and dirty."

"Oh, yes. Without a doubt."

I grin and roll my hips, finding the moist entrance of her pussy. "Then without any hesitation let's make this official. You're mine, Nakeyla Northwood." I thrust my hips forward and her head falls back. Her wolf lets off a howl and it is so fucking sexy I almost come.

But it's way too soon for that.

Pausing to focus and collect myself, I wait until my balls stop burning with my release. There's no way I'm depriving Keyla of her wish to be pinned down and thoroughly claimed.

"How does that feel?" I glance down at her distracted by the heaving rounds of her breasts. Sweet hell, this woman gets to me.

"So full." Her eyes are wide with wonder, her smile a sexy delight. "I feel full and stretched and so incredibly hungry. How am I going to survive this?"

I chuckle. "We'll have to lick and suck and fuck one another until your hunger is sated. That's how it works."

She bites her bottom lip and nods. "If that's what we've gotta do, then let's get to it. What have you got in you, Prince Creed?"

My heart pounds in my chest as I brace my palms on the ground and start pumping my hips. "Oh, I've got lots. I've got years of pent-up energy, Little Wolf."

The slap of flesh-on-flesh mixes with the feminine sounds Keyla makes when being thoroughly claimed. It's erotic as fuck and it spurs me on harder.

What starts as a controlled and playful rhythm quickly becomes more. Keyla lifts her legs and digs her heels into the fleshy globes of my ass and uses the leverage to quicken my thrusts.

She's wild. And she's right. She doesn't want slow and precious. She wants to be consumed.

The two of us devolve into a frantic mass of groping hands and slapping bodies and silver and brown hair twining together. I'm not gentle and she doesn't want me to be. She's burning for it so hotly, I'm not sure I'll be able to put that fire out.

I'll die trying.

"Creed... yes!" she screams, and her muscles constrict around my cock, milking me with the force of her tight, virgin pussy. "More. Harder. I want everything."

Nonono... I don't want to go off but she's too much. *Fucking hell.*

I grunt and pitch forward, my hips locking as my world shatters and the universe's claim takes hold.

Absently, I feel the burn in my palm and my mind is bombarded with a surge of power. My connection to her is locked into place and I feel the rightness of it.

"Mine," she growls, her eyes glowing gold with her wolf. "You are mine, Creed Thornebane."

And yeah, being claimed by a powerful, alpha female wolf is too fucking sexy.

~

Keyla

The power of our searing bond locks into place and steals my breath. This male... this stunning, powerful, displaced prince is mine. And I'm glad. His skin, bare of hair, is as smooth as exotic silk covering his rugged build beneath. I run my hands down the outside of his thighs gripping my fingertips into his flesh.

"More," I say, my hunger returning in a hot rush. "I need you again."

His cock is still as hard as a granite column inside me even after his release. Is that normal?

"On your knees, Little Wolf." He withdraws from me and I miss the fullness of him immediately. Thankfully, the loss is short-lived. With firm hands on my hips, he rolls me onto my hands and knees and positions himself behind me. "Still hard and dirty?"

"Yes, please." My words come out too rushed and needy to hide my excitement.

I want all the positions. All the sex.

Creed's hand grips my hip as his fingers play in the moist mess we've made. "Look how your pussy weeps for me."

I laugh. "I'm a wolf. I don't have a pussy... call it my puppy."

Now it's his turn to laugh. "Alright. I'm going to fuck this puppy until you scream out my name again."

"Perfect."

Bracing my palms on the ground, I lock my elbows and push back as he enters me from behind. My breasts sway forward, my nipples budded tight as his sac tickles my thighs. My insides welcome him and I honestly don't know how I'm going to live a normal life ever again. I want to be naked and having sex every moment for the rest of my life.

After a couple of entries slicking things up, he pushes harder and faster. Creed's hips hit my ass, and I swear he'll push through my belly. He's thick and hard and I feel every blessed inch as he pushes and retreats.

"I think I could live and die, fucking you."

Laughter bubbles up my throat. "Were you reading my mind?"

Both hands grip my hips and now he's really picking up the

rhythm of his strokes. "No, but if you're game there is a little mind trick I'd like to share with you. It'll take the sex up a notch."

I'm growling, meeting his strokes pound for pound, my next release building in a slow and steady climb. "Will we survive if we take it up a notch? My wolf is a wild mass of wanton hunger as it is."

His chuckle zings straight to my groin and my wolf pants, clawing for more. "Is that a yes?"

The slide and glide of him entering and retreating is so decadent I drop my head and groan. "Yes, anything. You have free rein to pleasure me any way you want."

"An open offer. How trusting." I hear the amusement in his voice, but I also hear the awe. "This will be intense, but remember, you're safe with me. I've got you."

Since we're in his dreamwalking sequence anyway, I'm not worried. What could be so—

Something unlocks in my mind and then not only am I feeling his cock sliding within me, but I'm sharing his sensations. I feel the pulse and the pull as I squeeze him and how his heart is hammering in his chest. I feel his pleasure burning low in his groin and how much power he's still holding back. I feel his joy at feeling my pleasure and how much this connection feeds his powers.

The merging happens in an instant.

We are one, body, mind, and soul.

I flip my hair back and look at him over my shoulder. "All of it," I breathe, groaning as my next orgasm is ebbing forward. "Give me all of it or I might die."

Bruising fingers tighten on my hips and he lets loose. The *slap, slap, slap* of flesh-on-flesh rings in the air. It's mixed with his grunts and my breathless panting. Pleasure is everywhere.

My fingers claw into the moss as a piercing howl tears from my throat.

This is what I wanted.

This is what my wolf has needed.

But it's not just me. Creed is free. For the first time in years, the anger and betrayal aren't pushing him down and he is alive. His cells are firing, and his body is thrumming with power and energy.

The sex is punishing and I'm going to be sore, but it's perfect.

It's everything.

I shout as his hips lock forward and my body detonates. Minds linked, I feel as the burning pressure explodes from deep in his core and the two of us are catapulted beyond the reality of our bodies.

We are nothing but light and sound. Heat and touch.

The two of us collapse to the mossy ground in a tangled heap of sweaty limbs and heaving lungs. With the heat of the sun on us, I'm warm inside and out.

Creed rolls to his side and curls around me, running his tongue over the round of my shoulder before kissing along my collarbone.

Sometime later, I have no idea how long, he closes the mind link connection and eases out of me. He nips the tender flesh of my neck and flops back onto the ground beside me. "Not bad for a first encounter."

I giggle and close my eyes. "Yeah. Not bad."

Doc

At first, when I woke up to Keyla's feminine moans, I forgot where we were and what happened over the past three days. In the comfort of my sleep-fogged mind, we're in my suite across the hall from Brant and his mates at the Prime Palace, and the two of us have stolen another night cuddling and shutting out the world.

But then her breath catches, and the groin-tightening scent of her arousal grips me.

My eyes pop wide and I reach over. Then it hits me. I can't touch her. Her searing is holding me at arm's reach, and she can't be touched...

By me, anyway.

And as I watch the two of them in their sleep, as impossible as it sounds, I'd bet my left nut they are having some kind of shared sexy dream.

When Keyla's wolf growls, Creed groans, and the two of them give off the mixed scents of sweat and sex.

How is that possible.

My bear is reeling and wants me to shake her and wake her up, but I can't.

Not only do I not want to touch her and wake her up screaming, but I also don't think it's my place. The two of them are sharing something and it's something incredibly personal and sexual.

When it finally ends, they fall still for a moment before their eyes flutter open simultaneously. Okay, that's twice they've done that and it's no less creepy.

Keyla stretches and holds her palm up to examine the brand. What was black is now midnight blue and the skin around the design looks much less sore and red. "It worked," she breathes.

Creed lifts his hand and the two of them examine his as well —same thing, different palm. "At least that much is settled. No more agony from being touched or the risk of dying from being separated.

Well, that's good. I'm glad about that except—

"So, it's done," I say, my voice gruff. "The two of you had sex while I was sleeping in the bed next to you? That's kind of twisted, isn't it?"

Keyla's half-masted gaze drops sideways to meet mine. "No. It was on the mental plane. Creed thought since you and I already promised ourselves physically that he wouldn't take that from us. Mating on the mental plane allowed us to complete the bonding so you can touch me again and claim me as we planned."

I hear what she's saying, and I understand that she's excited we can move forward but I just watched her having erotic dream sex with another guy.

Am I supposed to be okay with that?

"Doc? Why are you growling at me? I thought you and Creed talked."

"We did," Creed says, rolling onto his side. We're all still fully dressed from when we rushed Keyla in to reconnect with Creed, but dammit the man oozes sexuality. Well, why wouldn't he?

He just had sex with my girl.

"I'll give the two of you a moment," Creed says, rolling to sit up.

Keyla shakes her head, her eyes glassing up. "No. You stay, *I'll* go. I'll go have a shower and get ready for our day. Your sister still needs finding and us uniting hasn't stopped the beacon from buzzing in my head and burning in my blood, so there's more to do."

Yep. Just time to stop and have magical mind sex with your destined mate and then back to it.

Keyla pauses for a moment and pegs me with a heart-breaking glare. "I'm disappointed, Bear. I smell the hostility and judgment and I don't appreciate it. We couldn't be together until Creed and I acknowledged the universe's bonding, so we did that. We couldn't be together unless Creed agreed to bring you into our union, and he did that. Stop looking at me like I've left you out in the cold. Everything I've done the past three days has been to find my way back to you."

Before I have a chance to reply, she shakes her head and rolls off the bed. Standing in the massive and elegant suite, she stops and looks around. "Creed? Where am I going?"

He gets up and presses a hand to the small of her back, ushering her around the bed and through a door on the wall behind the bed. He spends a moment in there with her and comes back once the hiss of water starts.

When he returns, he stands at the edge of the bed and scowls. "Did I miss something? Didn't we decide it was going to be the three of us? Didn't we both want to make her happy?"

I curse and roll to my feet. "Of course, I want her to be happy."

He looks at me and then back toward the bathroom door. "You see, I completely missed that. What I saw was you being a selfish prick and making her feel bad about things she has no control over."

I raise my finger and my bear lets off a growl. "Maybe you could give me one fucking minute to wrap my head around you mating the woman I love before you judge me for not liking it."

"Or maybe the whole idea of the three of us in a relationship was a bad idea from the start. The universe gave her to me not you. If sharing is a problem with you, don't worry, I'll make her very happy. You can go."

I follow the direction of his pointing finger and take my exit. Storming out of his bedroom, I navigate his living quarters and leave his suite. By the time I get to the corridor, my bear is losing his shit.

I slam the door behind me and roar. My voice tears from my throat and vibrates against the walls.

Rhylan practically tears the door off its hinges across the hall as Brant and Kotah come flying out of the door down the hall.

"What's wrong?" Rhylan asks, searching the corridor. "What the slecking hell was that about?"

"Fuck off, dragon. It's personal." I turn toward Brant's room, stomp up the hall, and they make way so I can take refuge inside.

"I suppose good morning would be a waste of a greeting," Brant says. "How about what the holy fuck?"

I'm pacing the guest room they're in and I'm losing steam. "Last night I thought I won the fucking lottery. Keyla was back and alive and apparently, she talked Creed into taking me on as a third. He said Keyla is in love with me and is in danger and thought my skills and my commitment to her made sense."

"That's fantastic," Brant says, "so why do you have a burr up your ass?"

"Because she's *mine*. She was supposed to be *mine*."

Kotah pulls on his pants and gives me a sympathetic gaze. "Do you want me to leave while you talk this out?"

I shake my head. "No. You're as much a part of this as he is. And honestly, I need you guys to help me understand how you do it. Keyla and Creed accepted their searing and I'm homicidal. How do you share Calli and not want to kill one another?"

Kotah looks at Brant and my brother bear shrugs. "I think, at first, we were all so focused on helping her understand her destiny that we would've done anything to make things right for her. After that, after we spent time together, we worked on developing our relationships with one another."

"What you guys have is incredible," I say, shaking my head. "But do you honestly think I can fall for Creed the way you guys fell for one another?"

"Why not?" Kotah asks. "From what I've seen he is principled, educated, and kind."

"And hot as fuck," Brant adds.

Kotah grins and nods. "Let's try not to think of him like that. He is, after all, now mated to my sister... which makes him our brother."

"Alright. Good point." Brant makes a face and turns his

attention toward me. "Keyla couldn't be with you until she completed the bond."

"I know that."

"She convinced Creed to accept you into their bed."

"I know that too."

"She loves you, dude. She's trying to make it work with the hand she's been dealt."

"I know all of this."

"Then what the fuck is your problem because if you say you're mad because you don't want to share, I'm going to nut punch you."

"Fuck you."

"No. Fuck you," Brant says. "Whether we're hitting it one-on-one or having a threesome or a free for all, there's no me or mine. *We* are mated. It is so far past awesome I can't even describe it. Did I have sex with Kotah all morning?"

Kotah grins. "Yes, you did."

"Hells yes, I did," he says, waggling his brow. "Did Jaxx and Hawk have Calli to themselves last night? Yes, they did. Do I think they got hot and horny?"

Kotah laughs. "Oh, they most certainly did."

I nod. "You gotta know it was hot as fuck too. And yeah, we weren't there but that doesn't matter. It's not a competition. There's enough love to go around."

"More than enough, actually," Kotah says.

I draw a deep breath and exhale. "I'm being a possessive asshole, aren't I?"

Kotah shrugs. "Honestly, you had a vision of what your future with my sister would look like and that was taken from you. It's different now, but it's not a bad thing. Having a husband and a wife mated to you is twice the happiness not half."

"Twice not half. That's profound, Wolf."

Kotah shrugs. "I have been known to wax philosophical."

"So," Brant says, "The only question now is what the hell you're doing in here with us when your mates don't know where you stand?"

I exhale a long breath and shake out my shoulders. "Good question. Hopefully, I wasn't too much of an ass and haven't blown it."

Brant snorts. "Trust me. If the number of blunders and missteps we took is any indication, you'll be fine. We were a train wreck at times." He looks at Kotah and shakes his head. "Not all of us. Kotah was our cinnamon roll perfection from minute one."

I clap my hands over my ears and head for the door. "La, la, la… thanks, guys. I'm outtie."

"Make things right, my brother… and give us forty before we head out. I'm craving cinnamon roll."

I get out the door as quickly as I can and don't look back. Damn, Brant. TMI my brother. Wicked TMI.

Creed has fallen back onto the bed by the time I return to the room. The water is running in the bathroom, so I turn and head that way.

He arches a silver brow at me as I pass. "You're an idiot. You know that, right?"

I growl and turn. "Look. You've been in the mix for three days. You don't know me or her or us."

His cocky chuckle grates on my nerves. "I'd say, at the moment, I know her better than you in a few areas."

There's no stopping my bear.

Creed had sex with my Keyla. Mine.

Before I get to the bed, he launches up onto his feet and meets me with equal hostility. I take my swing, but he ducks and lands a hard fist of knuckles to my gut.

I grip his shirt with both hands and push up in his grille. He grips mine and matches the hostility.

"If you're not in this with us, then bow out, Bear. This is my realm and she's my mate. We'll do great things together and I won't have you hurting her."

"Says the arrogant prick who doesn't know a thing about me and her."

"Maybe. But I know about *me* and her and I know what she hopes the three of us will be. Yesterday, when I spoke to you about it, you agreed to be part of this. What the fuck changed?"

You claimed her, you asshole. And by the thick feminine scent she gave off and the way she moaned, she wasn't simply completing the mating bond, she liked it.

It's takes everything I have not to say that.

What would be the point? It would just prove that I'm being an out-of-control jealous jerk.

"It's time to decide, Bear," Creed snaps, the two of us so close, the heat of his body is raising the hair on mine. "Either you're in this or you're not—I don't care which—but if you're in, get your head on straight."

He's right. I know he's right. Hell, I was coming in here to say and do exactly that before I saw him, and lost control of my bear's need to rip his head off.

"I'm *in*," I snap, meeting his ebony gaze so he can read my conviction. "My bear is reeling, but I understand where we are, and I'm determined to be part of it and make it work. Consider my head on straight."

Creed nods. "Good. Then fix things with our girl and mate her. We're not leaving this suite until you do. There's too much at stake to have you second-guessing where you fit in if things go down. Until this issue is settled, there's a chance you can be removed from the equation."

My bear lets off a warning growl and Creed shrugs. "This isn't your realm, Bear. There are dangers and enemies and duplicitous people here. If we are to be a trio, then get it done. I'll wash up in Honor's bathroom at the other end of the suite and give you two some privacy."

Creed steps back and I watch him leave.

Get it done? The guy's not much for candles and romance, is he? I see his point. There are forces at work.

Queen Laryssa thought she had him nailed down. Keyla—and by extension, Kotah—complicate her power play. Having me with them offers another set of eyes to watch their backs and another set of hands to fight.

Right. Now to convince Keyla.

I grab my duffle from by the bedroom door and head to the bathroom. I knock and wait. The water is off and she's shuffling around inside. "Babe? Can I come in?"

"That depends. Is your head out of your ass?"

I deserve that. "Yep. And my tail between my legs."

"Fine."

I expect to find her upset or maybe teary. Nope. Wrapped in a towel and bent over, she's hanging upside down rubbing a second towel between her palms, drying off her hair. Aggressively, drying off her hair.

"Sooo, you look pissed."

She flips up and glares at me. "Why shouldn't I be? I've done everything I can to make this right for everyone involved. There was no way for you and me to move forward without Creed and I moving forward first. You told him you wanted to try and then you got all growly?"

As her words bounce off the hard surfaces of the bathroom I lock down and take my licks. This is Keyla. She might look like a gentle flower but she's all feist and power. "You're right. I got bristled up and reacted badly. I was a jerk. I'm sorry."

She tucks the towel over the hanging rail and mutters something under her breath. "I thought you wanted us to be together."

"I do." I step fully into the bathroom and set my duffle onto the counter. After unzipping the top, I dig through the clothes I stuffed in there for her brush. "I was hurt and my bear got territorial."

"No argument." She crosses her arms over her chest and pegs me with a steely glare.

"Look at it from my side, babe. The woman of my heart is the perfect match for another man—a fucking prince for that matter. She runs off with him and almost dies. I can't touch her. I can't comfort her. Then, she has sex with the guy and from the outside looking in, she loved it and is happy the way things are working out."

Keyla shoves her branded palm into the air between us. "I was happy because our dreamwalk worked and the branding doesn't burn like my hand is in hot lava anymore. I was happy because Creed agreed to everything I asked of him, and you and I can mate. I was happy because when I woke up from nearly dying in a foreign realm, you were lying beside me, and I didn't feel so lost and alone."

Fuck me. "I'm sorry. I smelled your arousal and saw the effects of your dream sex and I wasn't in a charitable headspace. It was a hit to my ego to know you enjoyed having sex with another man."

She sighs. "Would you rather my first time with him not be enjoyable? I'm bound to him, Doc. I want to build a life like Kotah has with his fated mates. I won't apologize for that."

"And you shouldn't. It took a moment for my perspective to shift, but I got there. I spoke to Brant and Kotah and they set me straight on a few things."

"Yeah?"

"Yeah." I take her brush, step around her back, and start smoothing out the tangles. Her tension eases a little and I kiss her shoulder. "I was a jerk. That's over now, I promise. My bear freaked out and I felt left behind."

She meets my gaze in the reflection of the mirror and, like always, I melt a little. "I'm sorry you're hurting, Bear, but I am too. None of this was what I planned but the three of us were set on a path. You can either be on that path with us or not."

"I'm on it." I get to a particularly matted section of wet hair and use my other hand to hold it while I pull through the knots.

"What about your relationship with Creed?"

"I spoke to him last night about it and we're both open to see what happens. Anyone who spends five minutes with your brother and his mates can see the appeal. I'll work on it. I promise."

"Their quint is a beautiful thing. I want that."

I finish smoothing out her hair and set the brush on the counter, so my hands are free. "No more territorial bullshit, I promise."

"Good because I genuinely like and respect Creed and we've got important things to work out. There's no part of me that wants to leave you behind, but I also don't want you to be tied to something you don't want."

I dip my chin and open my arms. "I want it, beautiful. It's Team Trio for the win, I swear."

She comes to me with an ease and trust that makes my bear stretch languidly and calm the fuck down. "Creed says we don't leave this suite until the question is answered once and for all, so, Nakeyla Northwood, will you mate me?"

CHAPTER SEVENTEEN

Keyla

*W*ill I mate him? Of course, I will. I love him. I understand what he's been through. If he was suddenly bound to love another woman I would be hurt and terrified. And just like that, I understand his reaction. "Despite what you're thinking, you will never be demoted to second place because I'm fated to be with Creed, and I will never regret loving you because you're not a prince."

The relief that clouds his eyes tells me I got that exactly right.

"I love you, Bear, even growly and gruff. You are, and will always, be my first love, my first touch, my first mate." I step against his chest and hug him, thankful the violent pain of the searing doesn't ignite.

Doc's muscled arms wrap around me and he squishes me to his chest. "Then let's make it official. I'll give you the perfect romance mating night another time. Circumstances have changed."

"Nothing has changed for me. I've only ever needed *you* to make it perfect."

Dillan is a potent force as he takes my hand and leads me back to the bedroom. My heart is racing as I look around. "Did Creed leave?"

"He's in his sister's chambers at the other end of the suite. He left me with instructions to make things right with our girl and finish this mating issue. His exact words were 'get it done'."

I chuckle. That definitely sounds like Creed. He's far more direct and pragmatic than Doc. Having the two of them will be the best of both worlds. "I understand what he's saying. Me wanting you and worrying about you being taken from me drives me to distraction."

"Same."

"So, the wisest course *is* to get it done. Then we'll both find comfort in knowing we won't be torn apart."

He backs me up until my legs bump against the mattress. "Then, to ensure clear thinking going forward, if we must we must. A sacrifice made in order to go on to save the realm from an evil queen."

The teasing light of the gold specks dancing in his eyes infuses me with a joy I feared was lost. I unbutton his pants and shove the denim down his massive thighs, followed by the soft cotton of his boxers. "Am I allowed to enjoy myself as we seize our destiny?"

He steps out of his pants and pulls his shirt over his head. "I hope so. I intend to enjoy myself."

Good to know. My cheeks ache with my grin as I pluck the end of my towel free and unwrap myself. Dropping the thick, fluffy fabric to the floor, I guide his palm to the mound of my breast.

The rapt focus in his gaze has me nearly undone.

Sliding his hands around me, he fists my hair and tugs my

head back. My wolf ascends, my aggressive side liking the fierce urgency of his hold. He claims my mouth and I groan.

I love the way Doc kisses me.

It's like he needs to... like if he didn't have his mouth on mine, his bear would go crazy and kill someone.

I meet the intensity of his lips and tongue until the room shifts in a slow spin. Lightheaded, I give him my neck and breathe. It's happening.

After all my pleading and impatience, he's mine.

Doc explores my body with his hands and his mouth, nipping and nibbling my collarbone and shoulder. The soft rumble of his bear is a constant comfort as both man and animal weigh in on claiming their mate.

I can't wait any longer. Squirming sideways out of his embrace, I climb onto the bed and rise onto my knees in the center of the mattress. "What does my mighty warrior bear hunger for?"

His shoulders roll forward as he climbs onto the mattress, his weight tipping my balance to fall toward him. "Anything. Everything. It will take a lifetime to do to you all the things I want."

Great answer. I meet him chest to chest and this time it's me who instigates the groping and kissing. My greedy hands splayed across the corded muscle of his back pull him tight to my chest. His kiss is decadent but it's not enough... not nearly enough.

Easing away from his mouth, I press my palms on his chest and push him onto his back. His gaze is locked on the sway of my breasts as I climb up his body and rise over his hips.

"Do you mind if I take what I want first?"

He barks a laugh, and the vibration of his laughter bounces my seating. "There's no wrong answer here. You've always known what you wanted. I'm just really fucking glad it turned out to be me."

It is him. I want him so much it's consuming.

I'd never tell him this but being wild with Creed has made me even more lustful. It's also given me more confidence. I know what to expect and how things will feel and even a few things I like.

Reaching between the crux of my body, I grip his arousal and slide my fist from root to tip. My breath catches as he quivers in my hold. He's so hard, like stone... hot stone. I'm desperate to finally have him.

I stroke him once more before I lift my hips and shift to position his wide crest into the moist folds of my cleft. Glancing down at him from under heavy eyelids, I smile. "Last chance to run for home. You sure you want me for a lifetime?"

His jaw clenches. "I'm sure."

His cock is hot and so incredibly hard and my skin is alive with tingling heat. Every cell in my body throbs with the need to mate with this man.

Unlocking my knees, I slide down his shaft the short distance until I reach the resistance of my virginity. First sex isn't as painful for female wildlings as it is for humans because we heal fast and have a high pain tolerance. With our gazes locked, I thrust past the blockage and adjust to the momentary discomfort.

"Are you alright?" he whispers, gently squeezing my thighs.

"Perfectly."

This is what I've wanted for weeks—to climb into his lap and take him deep inside me. There's nothing to stop me now. I doubt anything could stop me. I crave him so acutely it burns in my blood.

I groan as I take him inside me inch by thick, heated inch. When I'm fully seated, I grind my hips and absorb the wicked fullness. Unbidden, I recall the sensation of Creed inside me as he lay over me and then how it felt to have him thrusting inside me from behind.

This is different—the same, but different.

My core clenches, gripping, tightening around him.

This. This is what I've wanted.

Doc's breath hisses out between clenched teeth. "Fuck, you're so tight."

"You shouldn't have made me wait so long." My words come out in more of a throaty gasp than voice but I don't care. Dillan Baskins is finally mine and I won't be embarrassed about how desperately I need him.

I will enjoy everything about this.

Remember every nuance of every sensation.

I close my eyes as he raises his palms and claims my breasts. His hands are warm, and I arc into his hold. Covering his hands with mine, I tilt my face toward the ceiling and ride him in a slow rise and fall of my hips.

"Damn, princess," he bites out, his teeth clenched. "You're killing me." His back arches, his breath quickening as if he's straining against his body's primal urge to mate.

Too bad. He made me wait.

It's his turn to suffer now.

The excitement of where this will end burns in my cells. Wildlings are sexual beings. And while taking many lovers is common practice for pretty much all wildlings except the royal family, taking a mate is a sacred and irreversible act.

Doc sits up and buries his mouth against my throat. The shift in position moves him inside me and he hits something interesting. I suck in a breath. I have no idea what he's rubbing against in there but it's so good.

I grip his cheeks and lift his mouth to mine. Working myself over his shaft, I rub that spot over and over, building myself into a frenzy.

Doc meets my kiss with the strength and virility of his animal side, every stroke of his tongue a thrust or parry to challenge mine.

My skin is flushed and damp with sweat, my core so hot and wet from gliding the length of his cock I'm ready to explode.

I love being in control. Why did I wait for him, ask him, beg him for this? How did I forget I am a predator? Wolves are playful and shy but also fierce and cunning.

Erotic sounds bombard me.

The guttural sounds he makes each time I sheathe him inside me and the sexy rumble of bear and wolf communicating their pleasure and possession.

Gripping his shoulders, I lean back, shifting in small degrees while I find that spot again and take advantage of it. My pulse races in my veins, my wolf is wild, and my intimate muscles are flexing and straining with the need to release.

"More," I gasp. "I want more."

Doc grips the soft flesh of my hips with bruising force, lifting and then plunging me up and down his cock at a frenzied pace.

It's the first time he's been anything but gentle with me and it's so hot to not be on his pedestal.

"Claim your mate, Bear. Like you mean it."

The room swirls out of focus as I'm twisted in the air and thrown onto my back with my bear still between my legs. My hair flies wild and fans out onto the crumpled sheets as Doc leverages his strength and takes over the thrusting.

Pleasure ripples through me with every hard and fast shove of his body into mine. He's plunging, gasping, pounding into me in a mind-numbing rush of heated desire. *Like this... I wanted him like this.*

My orgasm swirls like a violent storm about to touch down and then the keening hits. Sensations explode, stealing my control in exchange for raw pleasure. My breath catches in heady gasps. I clutch the sheets, my insides pulsing and grabbing his cock in greedy pulls.

Rocking his hips upward, Doc doesn't let up.

He impales me in long, deep plunges. He's more animal than man and it's beyond perfect... but it's also getting dangerous.

If he loses control, his bear will ascend.

His pace quickens, his breath escaping in short bursts. Heated waves of desire waft off him and it's all I can do to dig my fingernails into his shoulders and hold on.

"Fuck. I'm going to come so hard." Urgency laces his breath, his touch, his scent. I urge him on, calling for his bear's mark to claim me forever.

We're dripping with sweat, our bodies slicked together, the greedy pulse of my insides building and gripping him once again.

Yes. Again.

He buries his face in my neck, pinning me in place. It's too much. The scent of our sweat and sex. The sounds we make... The erotic sting of a second release erupts in a violent rush.

I cry out and the pumping stops.

Doc grips my hips and throws his head back. Neck stretched, muscles strained, his entire body shudders. He's brutally handsome... consumed by his release... and then I smell it.

All thought vanishes as his body spills inside me and he marks me as his own. The mating scent of a wildling male is strongly spicy and rich with aroma.

My wolf howls inside me and I sink into the covers the fading pulses of spent ecstasy still ebbing in my muscles. His heart pounds against my chest as I nuzzle the hollow of his neck.

"Hello, mate."

He chuckles and rolls off me and to the side, gathering me into his arms as the world comes back into focus. "Hello, mate."

∾

Creed

I've never been a voyeur before now, but what can I say, I was curious to see how the bear handled my female. Despite what Keyla said, Doc didn't seem to be fucking her gentle. Maybe they had a breakthrough. I'm of mixed feelings about that. I liked pulling the unbridled passions straw, while he got butterfly kisses and tender moments.

A shiver racks Keyla and I push off the doorframe of the bedroom and join the party. "You need to get dressed and dry your hair, Little Wolf. I don't want you to catch a chill."

The bear's growl draws my full attention and I shake my head. "Don't start with me, Bear. I didn't interrupt, in fact, I instigated this union."

"Sorry. That was my bear more than me."

"More than, but not only," I say, pointing out the distinction. "There's no going back now. We are three, so let's work on that, shall we?"

Keyla rolls to the side of the bed and grabs a towel off the floor. "I think it would help if you two kiss and make up."

Oh, hell. It was a lot easier talking about uniting as one than it is to be put on the spot to make it happen. I meet the smug upturn of her mouth and fight not to laugh. "I think all the mind-blowing sex you've had in the past few hours has gone to your head."

"Put up or shut up, my prince."

"Aren't you a sassy little minx," I laugh, taking the towel from her hands and wrapping it over her shoulders. "Time for you to get cleaned up. Our destiny awaits."

She pats my shoulder. "Fine, we'll revisit the idea once you've spent more than ten minutes together when you're not actively hostile."

"It would make for a better moment, I'm sure."

She waves to Doc and shuffles barefooted toward the bathroom. "Come with us, Bear. We'll get you set up for your shower."

Doc follows her across the room, a satisfied look on his face. "I think I can figure it out."

Her giggle does something sinful to me. To know she's happy makes me want to wrap her in my arms and devour her.

"You say that now," she says, "but Creed's bathtub is a strange combination of tub and carwash. You recline in the basin while the shower nozzles spray up and down your body. The fun part is the buffing cloths. They tickle as they spin and brush over your skin."

Doc frowns and then lowers his nose to his shoulder to perform a sniff test. "Well, I guess there's no avoiding it. Get me set up."

I take the lead and show him how the facilities work and then leave the two of them to clean up. It strikes me odd that after an entire lifetime of having this room to myself, two other people will be sharing it with me now.

We're going to need more drawers.

My gaze is drawn to the dresser against the wall, and locks on the top left drawer. When Bloom was killed, I stuffed everything of hers I had into that drawer.

Thinking about opening it and cleaning it out hurts.

In an act of sheer avoidance, I shift my attention to the bed and start smoothing things out.

"And you make your bed too?"

Keyla saunters out of the bathroom, dressed in gray khakis and a dark blue sweater. With Bloom on my mind, even looking at Keyla makes me feel disloyal.

"I admit," she says, braiding her hair as she approaches. "I do enjoy the housekeeping perks of being a royal."

I spend a couple of extra seconds fussing with the rolldown and smooth a hand over the sheet. Acknowledging the bond so that Keyla and I aren't in pain is one thing. Letting Bloom go and moving on is another.

When I don't think I can stall any longer, I offer her what I hope is a calm smile. "It was an easy fix since we slept on top of the bed with the coverlet. Anything more involved wouldn't be nearly as impressive. That I would've left to the staff."

She doesn't seem to pick up on my turmoil, so I take that as a win and grab the blanket to fold. "What's the name of your chamber attendant? If I bump into him or her, I want to address them properly."

She rounds the bed and collects the opposite end of the blanket and steps back to straighten things out. "The castle maintenance, cleaning, and stocking are handled by brownies. You won't see them. They prefer to work when no one is around. You can, however, get on their good side by leaving a little gift now and then with a note of thanks."

"Lovely. I'll be sure to do that. What kind of gift?"

As we step toward one another, we hold up our gathered ends and meet up. When she has a hold on them, I bend down and repeat the process. "A gift for a brownie can be as simple as a glass of milk with sweets or a bauble that glitters. They love shiny things."

"I'll make a mental note to stock up." Our knuckles touch as we finish, and her eyes meet mine. She stares for a moment and then ducks her head and turns to set the blanket on the bench at the end of the bed.

"I'm sorry about the eyes. They're hard to stomach, I know." No matter how much I didn't want a mate and didn't plan to care for her, for some idiotic reason it still hurts that she isn't happy with what she ended up with.

"I wasn't thinking that."

I bark a laugh and stride off to get dressed myself. "Of course, you were. I don't blame you. I can barely look at myself and it's been two years since the queen sentenced me with the curse of my beast."

I press my hand flat against the panel of my dressing room and the entire section of wall swings into my walk-in closet.

I feel Keyla following close behind me and when I grab a shirt and turn around, she's there, peering in and smiling. "Okay, I admit, I was focused on your eyes but not because they unnerve me. I was wondering about all you've suffered through."

I swallow. Even worse.

"I understand the eyes are part of her curse and the beast you shift into, but I don't understand why."

Facing her, I undress and make sure she doesn't see the scarring on my back. During sex with her on the mental plane, I made sure not to let her get behind me while my shirt was off.

My beast and the eyes are bad enough. I won't have her pitying me because the bitch crippled me by shearing off my wings.

"What is there to understand beyond her being a twisted bitch? The beast is under her control and each time I take that form it feels like I lose another piece of my soul to the thing."

She frowns. "She controls it?"

I nod. "Part of her plan to ensure my obedience. I'm pretty sure she and the blood witch can see out of the opal eyes of the beast when I'm in that form too."

"I'm sorry. That's despicable."

"On the list of insulting and invasive tactics Laryssa uses in her rule, it's pretty low."

"What do you know about the curse? Can it be broken? Is there a way to reverse things and rid yourself of the beast and her control?"

I shake my head. "I don't know."

"Do you know the name of the witch who cursed you? Maybe we can track her down and get answers."

I shake my head. "No. I'll never forget her face, but I don't have anything more to go on than that."

She crosses her arms against her chest and the stance pushes her breasts up and directly into my line of vision. She doesn't seem to realize how alluring she is.

"Maybe Lukas can help. He's a squire in the Guild of Mages and has astounding gifts. We can start there."

I don't like talking about what Laryssa's put me through. It makes me irritable... well, more irritable. With Doc being a dick and thought of Bloom and now talking about the curse and being Laryssa's pawn, I'm sinking into quite a mood.

In an effort to distract her and change the subject, I get back to dressing and strip off my pants. I half expect her to blush and turn away when I bare myself to her.

She doesn't.

Of course, she doesn't. I swear she's not intimidated by anything. When I toss the pants, she brightens and points to the heap of fabric in the corner. "Will the brownies return those clothes to Rhylan's room?"

Right. I forgot those were his. "Yes. They will take care of it."

"Creed? At the risk of upsetting you, may I ask you something that is none of my business?"

I finish pulling up a pair of boxers and select a pair of black fatigues from the hanging rail. "You can ask. With an introduction like that, until I hear it, I can't promise I won't be angry."

"Fair enough."

I finish with the fly and buckle and wait for her to speak. Whatever it is, she's not sure about bringing it up.

"When we laid together in the city tunnels, I smelled Rhylan on your skin. It was definitely a sexual scent and I wondered..."

Blood rushes from my head as my mind goes blank. I take a step back, bombarded by a million things. That's private... and dangerous she knows... and not something I'm proud of... and it could ruin Rhy.

Not that I care. Do I care? *Why* do I care?

"I'm sorry," she says, holding up her hands. "Please don't shut down. I'm not judging, and I realize there are a dozen reasons the two of you could be in that kind of situation. What I wondered was if you are alright?"

What the fuck does that mean?

I don't know what she sees in my expression, but she takes a couple of quick backward steps.

Fuck. Now she's afraid of me?

"Forget I asked," she says looking flushed. "Just know that whether the two of you were willing or if he forced the situation as some twisted torture, it doesn't matter to me. You're my mate now and my only thought is about your well-being."

Forced himself on me...

"I can't deal with this right now." Rushing past her, I make a straight shot for the outer rooms. "I need to arrange our escort. I'll be back."

Keyla

The door slams in the outer rooms of the suite and I tense. Doc is loping out of the bathroom with a spring in his step and a smile on his face. When the echo of anger reverberates through the suite, he freezes, making a face. "What did I miss?"

"I asked Creed about something personal, and in hindsight, it may have been too soon."

Doc waves that away. "I'm sure it wasn't you."

"Oh, it was definitely me. I think it'll be fine though. There's a learning curve to being mated. The idea of sharing our skeletons won't always be easy."

Doc waggles his brow and takes my hand. "Easy, no, but I bet it will be fun."

I'm relieved to see his demeanor has improved. "How was your shower?"

He chuckles. "Interesting. I think I should've bought her dinner first, though. I didn't know it would get so sexually inappropriate so quickly."

"Right?" I giggle and step in to hug him. "I'm sure she enjoyed her job of teasing and tickling all your dirty parts."

"I hope so. At least as much as I enjoyed it. Man, I bet this realm has the cleanest citizens ever."

Rhylan

I'm sitting at the table with my morning nourishment steaming in my mug when my door swings open and Creed storms in looking like he's been slugged in the nuts with something hard and pointy. "She knows. What the fuck am I supposed to say to her?"

I blow across the rim of my mug and set it on the table. "Close the door. More information. What's wrong?"

He turns back, closes us in, and drops his chin to glare at me through hooded eyes. "Keyla just asked about us having sex. She's worried you might've taken advantage of me on Laryssa's orders."

I stand with such force, my chair crashes back on the floor. "She thinks I raped you?"

He growls and runs his fingers through his long silver hair, shaking his head. "I don't think so. She smelled you on my skin the other night and is worried. She said she wasn't judging, she just wants me to be alright."

"How the slecking hell did she smell me on your skin. That was days ago."

"From what I gather, the heightened smell of wolf wildlings

is stronger than others."

I scan the interior of my suite, my mind a swirling battle-field. "She can't know. If Laryssa finds out... If Vik finds out..."

"I know. That doesn't change the fact that she already knows."

"Has she told anyone?"

"Not that I know of. She hasn't been alone with anyone except... oh, fuck, she's alone with her bear now and after I stormed out he might ask."

Creed bolts for the door and I curse and grab my shirt. Racing across the hall, I'm sliding my shoulders into my sleeves and buckling up as we enter the living room of the private residence.

Creed stops dead and I crash into him and knock him forward. Keyla and Doc are standing by the windows looking out onto the grounds. When we come crashing in, they turn looking alarmed.

The bear takes a protective stance between us and the white wolf. "Where's the fire, boys? What's up?"

Obviously, the two of us didn't think this through because what do we say? I curse and focus on buttoning up my shirt. This whole mating bullshit is Creed's mess.

Let him clean it up.

"The prince needs to speak with his wolf."

Keyla looks alarmed but doesn't hesitate to go into the other room with him. That leaves me with the bear. The bear who very recently had sex and mated with Keyla if my sense of smell is any good. Which it is.

Apparently just not as good as Keyla's.

So the mighty royal couple is now three... and they're discussing my role as the prince's sexual sparring partner. "How awkward is this whole situation?"

Doc lifts his chin and laughs. "I hear you. What the fuck, am I right?"

I take a deep breath and exhale. "The other night, tracking the two of them down, we made a pretty good team."

"Two like-minded men on the hunt for the ones we need most."

The ones we need most? I stomp forward, my temper flaring. "She told you? Slecking hell, that bitch of yours will get me killed."

Doc hits me like a juggernaut and pushes me back. "What did you call her."

"A bitch. A female canine. A nosy woman who needs to keep her fucking mouth shut."

I crash into the wall with enough force to break through the plaster and send artwork tumbling to the floor. A massive hand clamps across my throat, restricting my windpipe. Light flashes behind my eyes and my dragon ascends.

"Call her that again. I fucking dare you." The bear's animal is growling like a wild beast.

"Whoa. What's happening?" Creed's back and he's trying to pry the golden-eyed bear off me. "Dillan, stop. Don't. Please don't."

"Doc, let him go," Keyla says. "Whatever happened, let it go."

"He called you a bitch." The words tear out of his lips as a crowd gathers. "Twice."

The Wolf King, the bigger bear, and Vik come rushing inside. Vik is about to throw down when Brant grabs hold of his brother and hauls him off me. I sag to my knees and drop my head between my arms.

Slecking hell, bears might be as strong or stronger than dragons.

A gentle hand brushes the curtain of my hair back and then Keyla is peering at me with worry thick in her gaze. "Are you alright?"

"Why do you care?" Doc snaps. "He insulted you."

She shakes her head, and her chestnut mane brushes my

fingers. "There was a misunderstanding. I offended Rhylan and insulted him first. I'm sorry. I didn't mean any harm and I certainly didn't mean to start a war."

"It's my fault too." Creed clasps hands with me and helps me to a chair. "Keyla is protective and defensive about what I suffered in my imprisonment the past two years. If I had been more forthcoming with her, this wouldn't have happened."

Vik looks from me to Creed to Keyla. "You don't get to weigh in on something that has nothing to do with you, Wolf. Creed's imprisonment is Laryssa's decision and since she's our queen and not you, having your boyfriend strangle my brother is out of line."

Keyla looks at me and dips her chin. "Understood. I apologize. Nothing more will be said on the matter."

What does that mean? Did she or didn't she tell the bear? I glance over to where Brant has his arms out and is blocking Doc from us. Damn. Is that what mating does to a man. If so, keep it the hell away from me.

Creed runs his fingers through his hair and sends me a look that grabs me by my nuts. Is this what it'll be like now? Him sharing things with these two strangers and me being the asshole getting choked out? *She didn't say anything. I should've known she wouldn't. I'm sorry. I'm fucking this up.*

His voice in my head is new and far too intimate. I'm not sure what to do with the sensations it triggers in me. Especially not in the company of the room.

"Alright, if we can all regroup," the Wolf King says, taking charge of this mess. "Things to do. Places to go."

Creed nods. "I would like to give the brothers of my mates a tour of the city and explain the workings of our society."

Vik snorts and shuts that down. "What part of house arrest don't you get?"

Creed shakes his head. "Think about it, Vik. There are eyes watching. The rift is open and Kotah is here to make inroads with this realm. Laryssa securing positive relationships with the Northwoods is good for everyone. Locking me up in my suite does nobody any good. We should be out there, showing the citizens that Dornte is establishing allies with the other realm."

"Right you are, my son." The seven of us turn as Queen Laryssa steps through the open door. She scans the chaos of the room and a cool smile graces her lips. "And to that end, I believe a tour of Dornte is a wonderful idea. Vikarus, arrange the royal shuttle. We leave immediately."

My insides twist, but I don't let it show. I push down my anxiety and bow my head. "As you command, Majesty."

CHAPTER EIGHTEEN

Keyla

*W*e're a tense group of tour-goers. As the royal shuttle pulls away from the castle, Laryssa is plying Kotah with passive-aggressive influence to sway his opinion of her. Doc is still glaring at Rhy. Vik is glaring at Doc. Rhy is desperately avoiding eye contact with me and Creed. And, as usual, Brant is unaffected. He's pointing out the window and chatting about the sights.

You gotta love Brant.

I'm so sorry. I project my thoughts toward Creed, hoping I can initiate a conversation over his private mental channel. Most of what's going wrong on this shuttle from hell is my fault.

Creed slides his hand onto my thigh and shakes his head almost imperceptibly. *It's my fault. I was shocked, panicked, and a little embarrassed. I should've spoken with you instead of storming out.*

Calli once told me, when life gives you lemons, make sure you know who's eyes you're going to squirt them into before you squeeze.

He chuckles quietly to himself and that's all I'm going for.

I won't bring it up again. You can assure Rhylan I won't put either of you into any danger by making it an issue. I simply wanted to check on you.

He shifts his hand, so his branded palm is facing up. *I'm sorry it became more than that. I'm unaccustomed to people caring with no ulterior motive.*

I meet the design with my own and lace our fingers together. *That you are guarded is perfectly understandable considering what you've been through.*

It's over. Everything is changing now. I feel it.

All I feel is the burning in my blood, drawing us to wherever we're supposed to be, drawing me to you.

The contact of our joined hands is sending waves of sexual awakening straight to my core. I close my eyes and take a moment to adjust. I want him again.

It's only been a few hours since our time in the grotto, but my flesh aches for his touch. *I need to be naked with you again. My wolf is restless and hungry to be consumed by you again.*

He dips his head and brushes the shell of my ear with his lips. *I look forward to it.*

As my animal side revels in the anticipation of what is to come, I shift my attention to Doc. He's not growling but he's not happy either. I lace the fingers of my other hand with him. I *will* make this right for him.

We just need a little time.

I'll show him what I see in Creed, and I'll bring them together. I'll prove to him he's not a plus one but an equally important part of our mating.

"Young lovers," the queen says, smiling over at us. "I'm glad you're feeling better, my dear girl. I heard you were out of sorts yesterday."

I straighten and bow my chin. "Thank you for your concern, Majesty. Yes, being separated from Creed was dangerous and painful for both of us. There's much to learn about what it means to be soul seared mates."

She looks as if she's filing that information away for a later date. I let her think she has something on us. Too bad. Separation torture is now off the table.

"The reports I heard said you nearly died. Yet you seem fine now."

I nod. "Once Rhylan escorted us back to Creed's quarters we both recovered."

"And what were you doing in the city away from him in the first place?"

"The four of us, Kotah, Brant, Doc, and I went out into the city. We didn't realize there was a proximity restriction on our mating until we were out and about. Luckily, when Prince Creed collapsed in his quarters, Rhylan tracked us down and got us back to the castle before he perished as well."

The queen is an alarmingly gaunt and angular woman with aggressive icicle hair poking out from her head at odd angles. The salmon lipstick she's chosen for the outing is a terrible color next to her mauve skin.

Doesn't this realm have a royal cosmetician?

"Yes, well, that aligns with what I've heard of the event too. Though I'm still not certain why Prince Creed wasn't with you."

Rhylan and Vik are sending me daggered glares but it doesn't faze me. The enemy of my enemy is my friend. The dragon twins aren't any warmer toward the queen than we are.

"He wasn't feeling well. From what Doc could tell, the food Creed ate off our table in the clearing didn't sit well with his digestive system. It sent him back to the castle while we were still quite keen on exploring."

The queen shifts her gaze toward Dillan. "And you are certain he is well now?"

Doc nods. "All is well."

Creed squeezes my hand and winks at me. "I'm much

better. The stomach ailment was nothing next to the agony of separation. After the two of us were reunited, we slept through the rest of the day and all of the night and are much improved."

The shuttle stops and the queen looks around. "Why have we stopped?"

"That's my fault, Majesty." Brant rises from his seat and grabs one of the passenger rails as he moves to the side door of the shuttle bus. "I need to get back and check in with our mates or they'll worry something happened."

I hold out my hand to squeeze his in goodbye. "My love to the others."

Brant winks. "I'll tell them. Congratulations again on your mating, Princess. We'll see you soon."

The queen tilts her head. "You plan on returning?"

"Yeah. I won't be gone long. I'll assure them all is well and they can cancel the invasion plans."

I know Brant well enough to expect insouciance like that from him, but the queen looks like she might choke.

"You must excuse my mate," Kotah says, shifting to the front of his seat with a patient smile on his face. "He envisions himself quite a comedian. No one is planning to storm the realm. I merely instructed them if we didn't return in short order they were to prepare for hostile action. So, as you see, no need to worry."

The queen's glare drips with disdain. "Don't flatter yourself, young man. I'm not worried."

"Fun." I smile at Creed and Doc. "Isn't this fun?"

Brant chuckles and flashes me a wink. "Creed invited the quint to come and stay for a bit while Kotah and Hawk establish the portal bridge destinations with the other quadrants. Prepare to celebrate your mating Guardian quint style."

I bark a laugh. "Can anyone truly be prepared?'

"Good point. No, I guess not." Brant's chuckling as he steps out of the shuttle and jogs toward the round Colosseum building to portal back to our realm.

I squeeze Creed's hand and lean in to kiss his cheek. "I love that you invited them. Thank you. I'm excited for you to get to know them and show them around your realm."

But Creed isn't listening. His focus is locked on the distant horizon. I follow his gaze and goosebumps tingle over the surface of my skin. The beacon pulling us toward our future eased with the mating but it's back now.

And it's calling.

Creed stands and grabs one of the passenger rails by the side door. "Driver, hold. My wife desires a tour and there's no better way to explore the city than by foot. We'll get out and walk from here."

"Walk?" the queen sputters. "No. You will remain inside the shuttle and return to the castle."

Creed frowns. "We will return to the castle, you have my word, but first, I want to take the Wolf King and my mates to the archives and show them the war depictions. King Nakotah is a scholar and expressed interest in studying the history of the realm. Join us, Majesty. It will only take an hour or two to go through the exhibits."

The queen waves that away. "My time is too precious to wander through the past when I am busy sculpting the future. You may take your guests through the exhibits with Rhylan and Vikarus as your escorts."

Creed nods and dips his chin. "Thank you, Majesty. I look forward to telling you about our outing later."

"Shouldn't one of the dragons escort the queen back to the castle?" I ask. "My mother would never be caught in the city without a proper guard. Her being kidnapped and held captive last week proves anything can happen."

Rhylan nods and gets to his feet. "Vik, escort Queen Laryssa back to the castle and then you can meet us when you're done."

Vik's gaze narrows on his twin but he doesn't argue. "I'll contact you when I'm returning and you can give me your exact location."

Rhy steps out of the shuttle and into the midday foot traffic of Dornte citizens. Kotah, Doc, Creed, and I follow.

When the royal shuttle pulls away from the curb, Rhy looks at Creed and frowns. "Okay, so I bought you a few hours. There's no way you're interested in the archives. So, what's going on?"

Creed grins and points back toward the portal hub. "Destiny is calling and my mates and I are going to see where it's taking us."

AFTERWORD

~~ THE END ~~

Thank you for reading Dark Curse the sixth book in the Guardian's of the Fae Realms series and book one of Keyla's harem.
Claim book 7 – Dark Soul now.
If you are inclined to help a girl out, it would be amazing if you could leave a star rating or review.
If you want more, join my newsletter and be notified when new books launch and for all my news and sales!

Author Notes

Written on 03/14/2021

It's great to be back with the Guardians of the Fae Realms again and turning up the heat on my storytelling. For those of you who don't know, I write my sexy/steamy urban fantasy, paranormal, and sci-fi romance as JL Madore and my 'no sex' novels for the same genres but just closed door under the name Auburn Tempest. That pen name has had a great run lately with the Chronicles of an Urban Druid series and I focused on getting a book a month out in that series for three months.

It took me away from RH for a bit, but I'm happy to be back.

So, thank you for reading and continuing to spend time with Calli and Keyla and the men they can't help but love. There's plenty coming at Creed and Keyla and Doc's going to be right there with them putting it all together.

Hugs to all,

JL

Find Me

My Direct Sales Site: Shopify
Web page – www.jlmadore.com
Email – jlmadorewrites@gmail.com
Newsletter – JL Series Updates

ALSO BY JL MADORE

JL's Reverse Harem Titles

Guardians of the Fae Realms

Guardians of the Phoenix – Calli's Harem

Book 1 – Rise of the Phoenix

Book 2 – Wolf's Soul

Book 3 – Bear's Strength

Book 4 – Hawk's Heart

Book 5 – Jaguar's Passion

Darkness Calls – Keyla's harem

Book 6 – Dark Curse

Book 7 – Dark Soul

Book 8 – Dark Crown

Guardians of the Crown – Honor's Harem

Book 9 – Honor Restored

Book 10 – Honor Guards

Book 11 – Honor Bound

Book 12 – Honor Empowered

Rise of the Amberloq – Lark's Harem

Book 13 – Find the Fallen

Book 14 – Rise from Ruin

Book 15 – Trust and Triumph

Exemplar Hall

Exemplar Hall – Jesse's Harem

Book 1 – Captured by the Magi

Book 2 – Jesse and the Magi Vault

Book 3 – The Makings of a Magi Knight

Book 4 – Clash with the Magi Council

Book 5 – The Unstoppable Storme

Club Sanguine

Book 1 – Moonstone Maelstrom

Book 2 - Sunstone Sacrifice

JL's More Traditional M/F, M/M, or Menage

The Watchers of the Gray Series (Paranormal)

Book 1 – Watcher Untethered – Zander

Book 2 – Watcher Redeemed – Kyrian

Book 3 – Watcher Reborn – Danel

Book 4 – Watcher Divided – Phoenix

Book 5 – Watcher United – Seth

Book 6 – Watcher Compelled – Bo

Book 7 – Watcher Unfeigned – Brennus

Book 8 – Watcher Exposed – Taharqa

The Scourge Survivor Series (Fantasy)

Book 1 – Blaze Ignites

Book 2 – Ursa Unearthed

Book 3 – Torrent of Tears

Book 4 – Blind Spirit

Book 5 – Fate's Journey

Book 6 – Savage Love – epilogue novella

Aliens of Atlantis Series (Sci-Fi)

Book 1 – Taryn's Tiderider

Book 2 – Kai's Captive

Book 3 – Alyandra's Shadow